WARPED GALAXIES

PLAGUE OF THE
NURGLINGS

STORIES FROM THE FAR FUTURE

WARPED GALAXIES

STORIES IN AN AGE OF FANTASY

REALM QUEST

WARHAMMER
ADVENTURES
STORIES FROM THE FAR FUTURE

WARPED GALAXIES

PLAGUE OF THE
NURGLINGS

See Warhammer Adventures on the internet at

warhammeradventures.com

Find out more about Games Workshop and the world of
Warhammer 40,000 and Warhammer Age of Sigmar at

games-workshop.com

Printed and bound by CPI Group (UK) Ltd, Croydon, CR0

CAVAN SCOTT

WARHAMMER ADVENTURES

First published in Great Britain in 2020 by
Warhammer Publishing,
Willow Road,
Nottingham, NG7 2WS, UK.

10 9 8 7 6 5 4 3 2 1

Produced by Games Workshop in Nottingham.
Cover illustration by Cole Marchetti.
Internal illustrations by Dan Boultwood & Cole Marchetti.

A CIP record for this book is available from the British Library.

ISBN 13: 978 1 78999 036 2

Contents

The Imperium
of the Far Future

Life in the 41st millennium is hard.
Ruled by the Emperor of Mankind
from his Golden Throne on Terra,
humans have spread across the
galaxy, inhabiting millions of planets.
They have achieved so much, from
space travel to robotics, and yet
billions live in fear. The universe
seems a dangerous place, teeming
with alien horrors and dark powers.
But it is also a place bristling with
adventure and wonder, where battles
are won and heroes are forged.

CHAPTER ONE

Betrayal

Las-fire lanced from the *Profiteer*, striking the inquisitor's ship. Fire blossomed across the viewscreen, the sound of the impact reverberating around the flight deck.

'Have you seen enough?'

Zelia's eyes dropped from the hololith. 'Yes,' she said quietly, and the recording of the battle fizzled out.

'The inquisitor was telling the truth,' intoned Corlak, Jeremias's loyal servo-skull, as its tentacle-like mechadendrites manipulated the ship's controls. 'Captain Harleen Amity opened fire on the *Zealot's Heart.*'

'I realise this must be a shock to you,' said Inquisitor Jeremias from his high-backed command chair. He was immaculately dressed in a long coat, the mask that covered half of his face expertly polished, no doubt by Corlak. Zelia and her friends, on the other hand, were in a terrible state. Jeremias had rescued them from a battle between bloodthirsty Orks and rampaging monsters, scooping them up in a teleporter beam. They were smothered head to toe in mud and Orkish warpaint, their smeared faces betraying the dismay they all felt.

Jeremias was right – the revelation that Captain Amity had apparently abandoned them on Weald had come as a surprise. In a very short time they had come to like the rogue trader – to trust her – and for what? According to the inquisitor, she had attacked his ship as he came in to offer assistance, before rocketing into the stars.

At least Jeremias looked as though he understood their disappointment, regarding them with sympathy as he idly stroked the head of his ever-present cyber-mastiff, Grimm.

'Unfortunately,' he continued, 'none of this comes as a surprise to me. Harleen Amity is wanted for numerous crimes across the Imperium.'

'Like what?' Talen snapped, his arms crossed defensively across his chest. Of all of them, the former ganger had developed the closest bond with the apparently treacherous captain.

Jeremias shook his head. 'Where to begin?'

'You could begin with that business with the slaves, sire,' Corlak offered from the flight controls.

The inquisitor raised a gloved hand to silence the servo-skull. 'It was a rhetorical question.' He smiled apologetically at the children. 'You'll have to forgive my familiar. He can be a little... literal.'

Mekki's brow furrowed. 'What did he mean by slaves?'

Jeremias sighed. 'It's a sad story, I'm afraid. Amity sold an entire flotilla of refugees into slavery, over four thousand people by all accounts.'

Zelia's eyes widened. 'You're joking...'

'If only...' Jeremias replied. 'She had been hired to protect those poor people, and yet she betrayed them without a second thought. She lost her Warrant of Trade, of course. Her family were dishonoured and she became an outlaw.'

'Which is why she has no crew,' Zelia realised.

Jeremias raised a curious eyebrow. 'No crew?'

Zelia shook her head. 'Only a servitor...'

'Grunt,' Talen added.

Zelia shrugged. 'I always thought it was odd, but she said that she didn't need anyone.'

The inquisitor laughed, his voice echoing around the sterile flight deck.

'More like no one wanted anything to do with her.'

'But it doesn't make sense,' Talen said. 'She saved us. Looked after us.'

'Looked after this, you mean,' Jeremias said, pressing a button on his chair's arm. A hololith glimmered into view beside him. It was the Necron Diadem that they had been trying to return to Zelia's mother, the ancient relic that had caused a Necron war-fleet to destroy Talen's home planet.

The inquisitor pointed at the artefact. 'Amity yearns for revenge. With that Diadem she could destroy any planet under the Emperor's protection. That is what she and her accomplice wanted all along.'

'Her what?' Zelia asked. Surely he didn't mean Grunt?

'Her inside man. Or should I say... Jokaero.'

Now it was Mekki's turn to look amazed. 'You can't mean... Flegan-Pala...'

'The alien you took in on your travels? Of course I do. Didn't you think it was odd that a rare xenos just happened to hitch a ride on your escape pod? Tell me, how did Amity find you?'

'She followed our distress beacon,' Mekki replied.

'And who built the beacon?'

The Martian jutted out his chin. 'I did.'

'Based on your own designs?'

Mekki fell silent.

'Well?'

'It was Fleapit,' Talen said, replying for him. 'Mekki only helped.'

'He did slightly more than that,' Zelia insisted.

'No,' Mekki admitted. 'Talen Stormweaver is correct. I assisted, but the beacon was Flegan-Pala's design.'

'The beast was signalling for its mistress,' Jeremias concluded.

Zelia wasn't ready to accept that. 'That can't be right. There's no way he was working for her.' She felt her cheeks flush despite the chill of the flight deck. Nothing about this ship exuded warmth, neither the heating vents nor the surroundings, the obsidian walls so polished that they became mirrors, the various immaculate cogitator consoles. There was no character, no sense of who this inquisitor really was, the décor as blank as the mask Jeremias wore over half of his face. And here he sat, casting judgement on their friend. She couldn't let that stand.

'How can you be so sure?'

'Fleapit was on Targian when it was destroyed,' she said. 'He'd been held captive for years.'

'How do you know?'

The simple question confounded her. 'What?'

The leather of his chair squeaked as he sat back. 'How do you know the beast couldn't be working with her?'

'He told us?'

'You speak his language?'

'No, but Mekki…'

Her voice trailed off. Admitting that Mekki had attempted to forge a link to Fleapit's cybernetic implants probably wasn't a good idea, especially when talking to an inquisitor.

Jeremias leant forward in his chair, the grox-leather creaking. 'Mekki did what?'

'I… communicated with him,' Mekki admitted.

Jeremias's jaw clenched at the revelation, a vein throbbing at his temple. 'You are a psyker?'

The Martian shook his head. 'No. It was a data-exchange, nothing more. Flegan-Pala had dropped into a hibernation cycle.'

'Mekki tried to wake him up,' Talen said, jumping to his friend's defence.

Mekki nodded. 'And in the process, I learned a little about his past. Images, that is all.'

'And you believed them? You believed

a xenos?' The inquisitor looked at him sadly. 'Mekki, aliens cannot be trusted, especially a life form as devious as a Jokaero. Especially a life form in the employ of Harleen Amity.'

Zelia didn't want to believe any of this, her head spinning with every fresh revelation. Talen, on the other hand, seemed convinced.

'She played us all along,' the ganger muttered. 'And I trusted her... *we* trusted her.'

Jeremias rose from his chair and placed a comforting hand on Talen's shoulder. 'You shouldn't be so hard on yourself. Amity has deceived a great many people over the years.'

Talen didn't look ready to forgive himself. 'So what now?' he asked, wiping his nose on the back of his hand. 'Where do we find her?'

Jeremias smiled at them, displaying a row of perfect pearl-white teeth. 'Such spirit. You are remarkable children, really you are. To have endured so much at such a young age...' His hand slipped from Talen's shoulder and he marched towards his servo-skull. 'But Master Stormweaver is right – now is the time for action. Corlak, how long until we arrive at Aparitus?'

'Within the hour, sire,' came the clipped reply.

'Excellent work as always, my friend.'

Zelia wasn't familiar with the name. 'Aparitus?'

The inquisitor double-checked the navigation console. 'A nearby forge world. I have a contact there who should be able to assist us.'

'A forge world?' Mekki repeated, a hint of concern creeping into his voice.

The inquisitor smiled at the Martian. 'Yes. You should feel right at home.'

'Why?' Talen asked.

'Forge worlds are factory planets,' Zelia explained, 'usually modelled on Mars.'

'Where I was born,' Mekki muttered darkly.

'You could sound happier about it...' Talen said, but this time Mekki didn't respond. He didn't even look up when, a few hours later, the *Zealot's Heart* dropped into Aparitus's thick atmosphere. The skies were a sickly yellow, the landscape dominated by gigantic manufactoria that belched dense smoke into the atmosphere.

Jeremias took control of the ship as they zoomed towards a towering metropolis, the smog-filled air crammed with transports that flitted from

building to building like bloat flies buzzing around spoiled meat. Corlak, meanwhile, fetched rebreathers for Zelia and the others, masks that fitted tightly over the mouth and nose linked to oxygen canisters that could be clipped to their clothes.

'These will provide oxygen for one hour,' the servo-skull told them. 'Most buildings on Aparitus filter the air, but the atmosphere outside is heavily polluted.'

The ship shuddered as Jeremias brought it down on a landing bay outside the city. 'Not that we should be spending much time pounding the streets,' the inquisitor said. 'We'll teleport directly to Nalos.'

'Your contact?' Talen asked.

Jeremias nodded. 'A tech-adept I have collaborated with on a number of occasions.' The inquisitor's boots clacked as he marched towards the teleporter, followed by Grimm and Corlak. Talen joined them on the pad, but Mekki hesitated.

'Come now,' the inquisitor said. 'We must hurry if we are to stop Amity.'

But Mekki didn't move, staring at the teleporter in trepidation.

'It's okay.' Zelia came close to him, stopping short of touching his arm. 'I didn't enjoy being scooped up by that thing either. But it'll be fine. We'll be together.'

Mekki took a deep breath and followed her to the teleporter.

'Ready?' Jeremias asked.

She nodded and Corlak activated the device. There was a hum, then a crackle, and then Zelia's body was thrown into a storm of light.

CHAPTER TWO

The Cognis

The first time Zelia had been teleported had been disorientating, but not unpleasant. She and her friends had been rescued by Jeremias from certain death on the Orks' planet, and the journey to the *Zealot's Heart* had been over in a literal flash.

This time was different. It was as if she had been plucked from the ship and pulled into a tornado. Lights flashed in front of her eyes and her ears were assaulted by unearthly screams that clawed at her mind. Then, in the blink of a watering eye, it was over. She stumbled, released from the effects of teleportation, nearly falling flat on her face. She blundered into Talen, who gulped air in an attempt not to be sick.

'That was rough,' he croaked.

She could only nod in response, her throat parched.

Jeremias's deep voice cut through the fog in her head. 'Every journey through the warp is different. Some are more traumatic than others.'

'The warp?' Talen parroted, glancing at Zelia. 'You said travelling through the warp was dangerous.'

She had, back on the refugee ship from Targian. Zelia felt a stab of regret at how confident she had been back then, how superior she'd felt compared to Talen, who had never headed into space before. How quickly things changed.

'It can be,' Jeremias said, not giving her the chance to reply. 'But short journeys shouldn't leave too many scars, either physically or psychologically.'

'That's comforting.' Talen peered at Zelia. 'You okay?'

She nodded, stepping off a teleportation pad as grimy as the *Zealot's Heart* had been pristine. They had materialised in a gloomy corridor, the air stale but breathable.

'Is this where your friend lives?' she managed to rasp.

Jeremias looked around them, his face twisted with distaste. 'I said he was a contact, not a friend, although I've no idea why we didn't appear in his workshop. Corlak?'

The servo-skull hovered over. 'The teleportation corridor was diverted here.'

'To the hallway?'

'Apparently so, sire.'

'Then we will need to walk,' Jeremias said, striding towards a flight of iron stairs that rose up in front of a heavy door. The cyber-mastiff bounded up the steps, and Jeremias led the children up three steep flights. At the top was a passageway bathed in the greasy glow of a flickering lume-globe.

Talen screwed up his nose. 'This place makes Rhal Rata look good.'

Zelia had to agree. The metal walls were tarnished and the corridor smelled of oil and sweat. There were scum-rat droppings on the floor and dusty spinnerwebs hanging from the low ceiling. It was stuffy too, making Zelia's shirt stick uncomfortably to her back. Jeremias strode ahead, heading towards an arched door at the end of the passageway. He looked so out of place here, his impeccable clothes at odds with the squalid surroundings.

The inquisitor stepped aside as they reached the door, Corlak sweeping past to rap on the metal with a mechanical frond.

'Open up for Jeremias Drayvan of the Emperor's Inquisition.'

Behind them, Jeremias sighed. 'Really, Corlak. There is no need to be so formal. Nalos is expecting us.'

Even so, when the door slid back, the

inquisitor's red-robed contact dropped into a deep bow, his hunched back cracking. 'Inquisitor,' the adept wheezed in a thin voice. 'It is good to see you again.'

Jeremias didn't smile. 'And you, although I wonder why I found myself delivered into a dingy corridor rather than your chambers?'

Nalos wrung his gnarled hands together. 'I apologise for the inconvenience, sire. I disconnected the teleporter array in my workshop for security reasons. I didn't want any... unexpected visitors.'

The inquisitor's eyebrows shot up. 'I trust you aren't talking about me?'

'No, my lord. Of course not. I meant my fellow adepts. They have become... curious of late.'

'About your work?'

'Yes, sire.'

The inquisitor *hmmed* and ushered Zelia and the others inside.

'What kind of work?' she asked as

Corlak shut the door behind them.

Nalos shot a glance at the inquisitor. 'You brought children?'

Jeremias regarded the bedraggled bunch with something resembling, but not quite achieving, paternal pride. 'Extraordinary children, who have suffered much at the hands of the universe.'

'You have a kind heart, sire,' Nalos fawned, but the inquisitor waved away the comment dismissively.

'He didn't answer your question,' Talen whispered to Zelia.

She shook her head. 'No, he didn't.'

To say the workshop was cluttered was an understatement. Benches were scattered randomly around the cramped room, their surfaces piled high with the kind of gizmos that usually piqued Mekki's interest, although for some reason the Martian was hanging back. He didn't even seem interested in the flashing cogitator terminals that covered the walls or the screens that scrolled

with an endless
stream of data.

Zelia realised that
she had never seen
Mekki with one
of his own people.
Nalos wore scarlet
robes trimmed with
gold, and much of
his haggard face was
hidden behind a stark
metal grille that
covered his mouth
and nose. His eyes
had been replaced by
glowing red irises and
he stooped beneath
the weight of a dozen
or so mechanical arms
that were fixed to an
arthritic back. His
gnarled hands were
covered in metal rings
and his feet replaced
by curved metal claws.

Only the skin around his bionic eyes was exposed, his head cowled by a thick hood, but there was no mistaking the curiosity with which he peered at Mekki.

'What can I do for you, sire?' he asked, turning his attention back to the inquisitor.

'I have need of your talents,' Jeremias replied. 'In particular, your psychic amplifier.'

That was a surprise. Zelia had heard about psykers – beings who could project their thoughts or read minds – but, to her knowledge, had never met one.

Nalos's augmented eyes flicked towards them. 'And what of the children?'

'They are assisting with my enquiries. I am searching for a villain who seeks to bring ruin to the Imperium.'

Nalos snorted. 'Such a thing isn't possible.'

'Usually I would agree, but unfortunately our quarry has a weapon in her possession that could bring about our destruction if it was left unchecked.'

'The Omnissiah protect us,' Nalos muttered, hobbling towards an adjoining room. The door opened and the old adept led them into a chamber with a strange-looking throne at its centre. Not unlike Jeremias's command chair on the *Zealot's Heart*, it sat beneath a web of thick cables and chains that suspended a spiked metal crown which looked worryingly like a clawed hand. A second chair of a similar design was pushed against the wall, an identical cluster of equipment dangling above its high back. A solitary terminal sat to the right of the room, next to a door that Zelia assumed led through to the tech-adept's living quarters. Dust motes danced in the flickering light of candelabras that floated on buzzing hover-pads, the flames' soft glow giving the chamber the reverential air of a chapel or sanctuary.

The tech-adept busied himself around

the terminal as Jeremias strode over to the chair and ran a gloved hand through the hanging cables.

'You have made improvements, I see.'

The cowled figure nodded. 'I have expanded the range, as we discussed.'

'What is it?' Talen asked.

Jeremias smiled at the ganger. 'You have an inquiring mind, Talen. I like that.' He stepped aside to allow a clearer view of the curious chair. 'This is the Cognis, a device to supplement the natural abilities of any psyker.'

'A psyker like you?' Zelia asked, suppressing a shiver as his crystal-blue eyes rested on her.

'I am blessed with certain gifts, yes. Is that a problem, Miss Lor?'

'Not if it helps us find Amity,' Talen butted in, a little too quickly for Zelia's liking.

'And that is the problem,' Jeremias acknowledged. 'To locate Captain Amity, I require something that belongs to her, a focus if you will.'

'Something like this?' Talen said, pulling a four-pointed compass from his vest.

'That's one of Amity's brooches,' Zelia said. 'When did you get that?'

'When we were attacked by Nettle-Nekk's sniffler,' Talen told her. 'Watch this.' He spun the star on his finger and it lifted into the air, the metal glowing with bright light.

'How illuminating,' Jeremias said, reaching out for the spinning star. 'May I?' He plucked the device from the air, turning it over in his hands.

'Will that be sufficient?' Nalos asked.

'Yes,' Jeremias nodded. 'This is perfect. Well done, Talen.'

The ganger grinned. 'Not a problem.'

'But how will it help you find her?' Zelia asked.

Jeremias pushed aside the tails of his coat and sat in the chair. 'I have the ability to track people through items they have recently touched.' He placed the compass on the arm of the seat and removed a leather glove, which he passed to Corlak. 'Think of it as a bloodhound following a trail. It's how I found you.'

Zelia frowned. 'Really? Using what?'

Jeremias ignored the question as Nalos lowered the crown over the inquisitor's head. Zelia couldn't help but notice the look of discomfort that flashed across his usually stoic face as little metal prongs snapped down like pointed insect legs to clamp onto his forehead, holding the apparatus in place.

'Doesn't that hurt?' Talen asked.

'They do not pierce the skin,' the adept snapped in reply.

'That's not what I asked.'

'There is no need to concern yourself on my account, boy,' Jeremias told him before shifting his attention to the tech-adept. 'Are we ready?'

'Indeed we are, sire,' Nalos wheezed, hobbling back to the terminal. 'Nobody touch anything. Nobody at all.'

'Do you think he means us?' Talen whispered to Zelia as Grimm began to growl. The metal dog was hunched as if about to pounce.

'What's wrong with him?'

'Grimm gets... protective whenever I attempt this,' Jeremias said as lights flashed on the helmet. 'It is nothing to worry about.'

Zelia wasn't convinced. The cyber-mastiff looked ready to rip the inquisitor apart. The cables crackled with lightning as Nalos flicked switches and twisted dials. Zelia felt the hairs on her arms bristle, nausea rising in her chest.

'What's happening?'

'The Cognis is amplifying my mind,' Jeremias replied, his voice echoing as if they were suddenly in a much larger chamber. He was staring ahead, looking straight at them as he reached for the compass.

No. That wasn't right. He wasn't looking at them, he was looking *through* them, as if they weren't even there.

Grimm's rumbling growl intensified, to be replaced by a harsh bark as the inquisitor's fingers curled around the brooch, his eyes rolling back in their sockets.

'Ugh,' Talen groaned, holding his head. Zelia turned to ask him if he was all right before losing her balance. She stumbled, only to be caught by Mekki.

'What's happening?' Zelia stammered, her head throbbing in time to the energy that danced along the cables.

'The inquisitor is projecting his mind beyond the confines of Aparitus,' Nalos intoned as he manipulated the controls. 'His consciousness is stretching across the void.'

'It hurts,' Talen gasped, gripping his head as if he was trying to stop his brain from escaping its skull. Zelia could sympathise. Her own head felt as though it was about to explode. The pressure was intense.

'More power,' Jeremias shouted over

Grimm's frantic barking. 'I need more.'

Zelia's knees buckled and she collapsed to the floor, her mind on fire. Colours danced across her vision. Colours she had never seen before. Colours that shouldn't even exist.

'Stop...' she pleaded, clasping her hands over her ears. There was so much noise, pressing down on her, filling her mind. The bark of the cyber-mastiff. The screech of the machinery. Jeremias calling for more power. Nalos shouting that they needed to shut down the machine.

Yes, Zelia thought, *shut it all down. Please.*

She looked up at the inquisitor and screamed. Jeremias sat in the chair, his hand clenched around the lume-compass, a shadow rising up behind him. The shadow was like every nightmare she had ever experienced rolled into one, a disgusting mound of flesh with a wide drooling mouth. Its skin was the colour of rotting fruit, and broken antlers sprouted from its bloated head. When Jeremias spoke, it spoke too, its voice deep and wet and diseased.

'More power. More power now!'

Zelia couldn't drag her eyes away from the vision, even though the sight of it made her sick to her stomach. The hideous face split into a leering smile, pustules blooming over the spectre's vile flesh.

'Give me more!'

She heard the tech-adept argue, only to be overruled, Corlak barging Nalos aside to twist a dial. The pressure in her head intensified, the impossible colours blurring, the monster behind Jeremias swelling like a blister ready to burst.

'More power,' the inquisitor bellowed. 'More po—'

Sparks rained down from the web of cables and Jeremias arched his back in the chair. The apparition screamed and so did Zelia. She screamed and screamed until everything went dark.

CHAPTER THREE

Heretic

'Zelia? Zelia, wake up! Can you hear me?'

She could hear, but couldn't respond. She didn't want to. Her head felt as though it had split in two. Something cold and hard was pressed against her cheek. It took her a moment to realise she was lying on a grimy steel floor. But which floor? And who was that calling her name? She recognised the voice, but couldn't think of his name. She was having enough trouble remembering her own.

'Zelia!'

'Okay, okay,' she slurred, trying to

push herself up. Her arms were like jelly.

'Here, let me help you.'

Strong hands pulled her up. Her eyes opened and for a moment she panicked, expecting her vision to be assaulted by alien colours. Instead, she was greeted by a painful yellow glare which softened into the flickering of floating candles. A face swam into focus. Closely cropped hair. Blue eyes. A scar through an eyebrow that was raised in concern.

'Talen,' she whispered. Yes. That was his name. Talen.

He breathed out in relief. 'Thank the Throne. I thought... well, you don't want to know what I thought. I couldn't wake you.'

He sat her up and she looked around. They were in Nalos's Cognis chamber, a figure slumped in a chair in front of them. Her eyes widened. It was Jeremias. She jumped to her feet, stumbling as a wave of dizziness swept over her.

The inquisitor wasn't moving.

'What happened?'

'It was the psychic amplifier,' Mekki said from somewhere behind her. She turned to peer quizzically at the Martian, gripping hold of Talen's arm to steady herself. 'It overloaded.'

'Overloaded?' she parroted, shaking her head. It felt as if it was full of mud. 'I saw...'

'You saw what?' Talen asked.

She wasn't sure. There had been colours definitely, weird and terrifying colours, but what else? A ghostly figure, looming up behind the inquisitor? She couldn't be sure. It was slipping away like a dream. She realised that Talen was speaking, and tried to concentrate on his words.

'Mekki says we were affected by the psychic amplifier,' he was saying. 'Like vibrations from an engine. They... confused us, clouding our minds.'

She looked back at Jeremias. 'Is he...'

'He lives,' Nalos wheezed from the controls. 'But the Cognis is damaged, possibly beyond repair.'

'No,' Jeremias rasped, making them jump. 'We must try again.'

'We cannot, sire,' Nalos argued. 'The psionic field has overloaded, the scry-emitters–'

'Will be fixed,' Jeremias growled, looking at Mekki with bloodshot eyes. 'You... You will assist Nalos. Repair the machine.'

Mekki hesitated, shaking his head. 'No... I...'

'You heard the inquisitor,' Corlak said, swooping towards the Martian, its pincers snapping like the claws of a corpse-crab. 'You will assist the tech-adept.'

Reluctantly, Mekki joined Nalos at the terminal, which was as blackened as the cables that snaked down from the ceiling.

Zelia took an uncertain step towards the inquisitor. 'What did you see?'

Jeremias looked as if he was having trouble lifting his head beneath the weight of the helmet. 'Nothing but Amity's face...' he panted. 'Mocking me. *Laughing* at me.'

'So you don't know where she is?'

It took a moment for the inquisitor to reply, every word an effort. 'She is nearby.'

'On Aparitus?'

'No. In the void. I could... sense that she was in flight.'

'And the Diadem?'

Jeremias shook his head, sweat flicking from his hair. The cyber-mastiff growled.

'Calm yourself, Grimm,' Jeremias wheezed. 'I am still myself.'

Zelia frowned. What did *that* mean?

'I thought my head was going to explode,' she said, more to herself than anyone else.

'Me too,' Talen said, and for the first time she realised how pale he looked. 'That was insane.'

'I apologise,' Jeremias breathed. 'It must have been psychic overspill. You must have experienced a little of the... discomfort I endure whenever I use my abilities.'

'You go through all that every time?' Talen asked.

The inquisitor's voice cracked. 'You have no idea. The torment I experience. The... things I see.'

Zelia shivered, but she didn't know why. Had she seen something herself? No. It was just her imagination. In front of them, Jeremias tried to sit up in the throne-like device.

'But my suffering is nothing when you consider the generosity of the Emperor. A small price to pay for the gifts bestowed on me.' The inquisitor looked to Nalos. 'How long until the next attempt?'

As the tech-adept burbled a reply, Zelia spotted the lume-compass at the inquisitor's feet. Talen saw it too, and bent down to recover it.

There was a chime from the workshop. Someone was at the outer threshold.

Jeremias looked up, still short of breath. 'Who is that?'

Nalos's optical implants whirred. 'I

cannot tell. The feedback has disrupted the pict-feeds.'

The inquisitor barked for Corlak to investigate. The servo-skull buzzed through the workshop and activated the door. It whooshed back to reveal a female Mechanicus adept flanked by three armoured guards. Their faces were hidden behind gas masks complete with luminescent goggles, their muscular frames bristling beneath scarlet robes – but all eyes were on the glowing arc rifles they held in their bionic hands.

'What is the meaning of this?' Corlak asked as the adept swept into the room, one of her robotic limbs swatting the servo-skull aside.

'Show yourself, Nalos,' she demanded. Her face was largely free of cybernetics. Unlike the other tech-adept, she stood tall, her writhing mechadendrites flexible and lithe like the tentacles of a kraken. Her eyes had yet to be replaced but their silver irises glittered as if lit from within.

'Quigox,' Nalos lisped as he hobbled from the Cognis chamber, blocking the doorway so she couldn't see Jeremias in the chair. 'You have no right to be here.' He glared at the tech-guards. 'And to bring skitarii to my workshop...'

'No right?' Her voice was mechanical, devoid of any emotion, her reply a matter of statement rather than a direct challenge. 'I am a servant of the Omnissiah. You are harbouring a renegade.'

'Says who?' asked Talen, stepping past the tech-adept.

Quigox's head snapped around to face him. 'You will be silent.'

'You've obviously never met me before.' As usual, Talen was trying to appear confident, but Zelia could hear the nerves behind his swagger. He ploughed on regardless. 'What do you mean by a renegade? Who are you talking about?'

The adept sniffed dismissively. 'I have installed pict-feeds in every building in this city. The deviant was seen entering

these chambers.' She raised a slender finger and pointed past him. 'And there he is.'

Talen turned to see Mekki standing beside Zelia in the doorway.

'You think Cog-Boy's a renegade?' Talen laughed. 'Trust me – Mekki's all about rules and regulations.'

'Yeah,' Zelia agreed, placing herself in front of the Martian. 'Mekki is as loyal as they come.'

'Is that what the liar has told you? What of his brand?'

'His what?'

The adept pointed at the circuitry moulded onto Mekki's skin.

'His electoos?' Talen asked. 'They help him commune with machine-spirits.'

Quigox took a step forward, the skitarii matching her step. 'They are the mark of the Innovatum Cult that spawned his criminal parents.'

Zelia searched Mekki's face for answers, but the Martian only glared at the adept. 'His... parents?'

'You must leave,' Nalos insisted.

'Not without the boy,' Quigox replied. 'He evaded justice on Mars. It is the duty of every adept to round up survivors of the Purge and deliver them for trial.'

'What is to say he is not *my* prisoner?' Nalos asked.

The skitarii's rifles swung up.

'You have a choice,' she said dispassionately. 'Either hand over the renegade or be cut down where you stand.'

CHAPTER FOUR

Protection

'We'll see about that,' Talen said, snatching a vibro-spanner from a nearby workbench. Stepping in front of Mekki, he brandished the makeshift weapon... only to have it blasted from his hand by a bolt of arc energy. He cried out, clutching his scorched hand.

Quigox struck, a mechanical tentacle darting forward like a viper. The pincers locked around the frame that protected Mekki's withered arm, pulling him in. Zelia grabbed for his other arm, only to be stopped in her tracks by the barrels of the guards' arc rifles swinging around to face her.

Talen wasn't so easily discouraged. He charged forward but was floored by a mechadendrite that took his feet from under him. He was flipped in the air to crash to the floor.

'You will stay down,' the tech-adept commanded. But before Talen could respond, Grimm launched itself from the Cognis chamber, soaring over the ganger's head to land on Quigox. The tech-adept fell back, the snarling cyber-mastiff pinning her to the ground. The skitarii swung around, ready to blast the robotic hound from their mistress, but she threw up a hand to stop them.

'No! Don't! You'll hit me.'

Her mechadendrites slammed down on Grimm's back, sharp pincers trying to drag the hound from her, but the animal clamped its jaws around the nearest tentacle. Grimm bit down, steel teeth shearing the mechadendrite in two. Oil spat from the severed arm while Quigox fought back, releasing

Mekki's arm in the frenzy.

'Zelia!' he called out and she scrabbled forward to yank him free.

They didn't get far. The nearest skitarius made a snatch for Mekki's backpack, pulling him from Zelia's grip. Catching Mekki in a headlock, the guard shoved his arc rifle in Zelia's face. She froze, staring into the glowing barrel as a voice boomed out behind them.

'That. Is. Enough!'

Jeremias stood in the doorway, showing little sign of his ordeal in the psychic amplifier. He was standing ramrod straight, his hair slicked back, his gaze strong and steady.

'These children are under my protection,' he announced. '*All* of them. Grimm, let the adept go.'

The cyber-mastiff released its prey, stalking back to the inquisitor. One of the skitarii went to help Quigox up, but she batted his robotic hand away, pushing herself up, the severed tentacle hanging uselessly from her back.

'This is none of your concern.'

'Not the concern of the Emperor's Inquisition?' Jeremias asked, his voice dangerously quiet. 'I decide what is my concern, not you. Perhaps I will decide that this *entire planet* is worthy of my concern. How would that be? Your forge world investigated? Every corner of every manufactorum examined in exhaustive detail. Imagine the delays. The missed quotas. The penalties that would bring.'

'You haven't the resources.'

Jeremias regarded her with contempt. 'Is that a challenge?'

The tech-adept hesitated, chrome-capped teeth grinding together before she finally relented.

'Release the heretic,' she hissed, repeating the instruction with more force when the skitarius failed to heed her command. 'Release him.'

Mekki scampered back to Zelia and Talen, who surrounded him in case

Quigox changed her mind.

'Thank you,' Jeremias said. 'I commend your dedication to the Adeptus Mechanicus. It will be noted in my official report. Make sure that's all I'm tempted to record.'

The threat in his voice was clear.

Quigox stalked from the workshop without another word, her tech-guards falling in behind.

As soon as they were gone, Jeremias slumped where he stood, nearly dropping to the floor. Talen jumped

forward to support the inquisitor before he could collapse.

'Are you all right?'

'It is nothing,' the inquisitor croaked. 'The Cognis has left me weakened, that is all.' His eyes dropped to a burn on Talen's palm where the spanner had been electrified. 'But you have injuries of your own.'

Talen flexed his fingers. 'This? It's nothing. I've felt worse from shock-sticks back home.'

Jeremias offered a weak smile. 'You are strong. That is good.'

'You better believe it,' Talen said, helping the inquisitor back to the Cognis device.

'We must hurry,' Jeremias said as he flopped into the chair. 'Quigox will not rest until she has her pincers on our Martian friend.' He glanced at Nalos, who was cowering nearby. 'Not that she should have known we were here in the first place...'

The tech-adept wrung his crooked

hands together. 'Quigox has electronic
eyes and ears everywhere. I thought
I had checked the building for spying
equipment, but...'

'But you failed.' Jeremias glanced
up at Mekki, who was still in the
workshop, Grimm standing guard at
the front door. 'Mekki, perhaps you and
Zelia could scan for scrying devices.'

'I will assist,' Corlak chirped, but the
inquisitor shook his head. 'No. You will
assist Nalos.'

'What about me?' Talen said.

'You will help me, my boy.'

Talen frowned. 'Me? How?'

Jeremias didn't answer, but looked
pointedly at Zelia and Mekki. 'The scan,
if you please...'

'Okay, okay,' Zelia mumbled,
reluctantly joining Mekki in the
workshop. The door closed behind them
and she heard a lock clunk into place.
Grimm reacted immediately, charging
back to scrabble at the shut door. It
didn't reopen.

'Ever felt locked out of a conversation?' Zelia said to Mekki, but the Martian didn't reply. She was about to ask if he was all right when she turned to find him already hard at work at a cogitator terminal.

With a sigh, Zelia joined him, not even sure what she could do to help.

CHAPTER FIVE

The Emperor's Will

Zelia wasn't the only one feeling like a spare part. In the Cognis chamber, Nalos was busy repairing the controls while Corlak fussed around the helmet which was again lowered around Jeremias's head. All Talen could do was listen to Grimm desperately trying to tear down the door.

'Should I let him in?' Talen asked.

Jeremias shook his head. 'No. He would only get in the way.'

I know the feeling, Talen thought.

'I was impressed by the way you stood up for your friend,' Jeremias said as his servo-skull scrutinised the cables.

'You are as brave as you are strong.'

Talen felt his cheeks burn. It had been a long time since anyone had praised him. 'I don't know about that.'

'It does make me wonder why such a gifted boy isn't serving in the Imperial Guard?'

Talen's blood turn to ice. Would Jeremias be so complimentary if he knew that Talen was a deserter, that he had ran away rather than join the Guard?

'I... I was *supposed* to sign up...'

'But you chose a different path.'

Talen nodded. 'Yes. I did. But I can explain–'

The inquisitor raised a hand to stop him. 'There is no need. I assume you ended up running with a gang.'

'Is it that obvious?'

Jeremias nodded at his chest. 'The patches are a bit of a giveaway.'

Talen glanced down at the symbol of the Runak Warriors sewn onto his vest. The stitching had started to fray,

the patch coming loose. Talen pressed
it flush against the green fabric of
the sleeveless jacket, the embroidered
twine rough against his fingers. His
life beneath the streets of Rhal Rata
seemed an eternity ago now.

When he looked up again, the
inquisitor had produced a small wooden
figure from his coat. He held it up,
watching Talen's expression.

'Yours, I presume.'

Talen rushed forward, snatching the
toy from the inquisitor's fingers. 'I

thought I'd lost it.'

Jeremias nodded. 'On the ice-planet. Zelia asked how I found you.'

Talen glanced up from the toy. 'My Guardsman?'

'It was obviously precious to you. I didn't need my psychic abilities to tell me that.'

Talen clasped the figure in his hand, a tear rolling down his cheek. He brushed it away, embarrassed. 'Sorry.'

'Don't be. I saw why you ran, Talen. Felt the pain when your brother didn't return from war. Witnessed the cruelty of your father.'

'He thought he knew best.'

'He was wrong. I for one am glad you didn't end up dying on a backwater planet, a lasrifle in your hands. You deserve better.'

Talen sniffed, slipping the soldier into his pocket. 'I don't know about that.'

'I do,' Jeremias insisted. 'I see great potential in you, Talen. We will do wonderful things together, you and I.

Would you like that?'

Talen pressed his hand against his pocket, feeling the edges of the soldier through the fabric. 'Yeah, I think I would. Thank you.'

'For what?'

'For keeping it safe for me.'

The inquisitor smiled. 'My pleasure. I mean what I say. Together, we will find Amity and recover the Diadem. Together, we will make things better.' He glanced at the control console. 'If Nalos ever gets it working again, that is...'

The tech-adept held up a ringed finger. 'I just need five more minutes, sire. Ten at the most.'

'I'm glad to hear it, Nalos,' Jeremias said. 'Young Master Stormweaver is keen to bring Captain Amity to justice, aren't you, Talen?'

Talen nodded. He had thought she was his friend, but had been mistaken. He wouldn't make the same mistake twice.

CHAPTER SIX

Trust

Zelia couldn't understand half the text that was scrolling on the viewscreen. Some was in Low Gothic, but the majority was in binaric with the odd passage in bizarre glyphs that she had never even seen before.

Beside her, Mekki had his haptic connectors attached to the cogitator's access ports, his free hand darting from one control panel to another.

'Have you found something?' she asked.

He didn't answer. She reached out to touch his arm but he snatched his hand away as if scolded.

'I-I'm sorry,' she said. 'I just want to help.'

The Martian went back to his work, and Zelia glanced at Grimm, who was still scrabbling at the door to the Cognis chamber.

'I don't think they're going to let you in,' she told the mechanical hound.

It ignored her too.

Zelia sighed, before finally recognising a word on the screen. 'Transmitter? Mekki, why are you trying to access a transmitter?'

'We need to get away from here,' he replied. 'It is not safe.'

'Because of Quigox?'

'Because of *everything*.'

She'd never heard him sounding so worried. 'Can you be a little more precise?'

Mekki looked up at her. 'I do not trust them, Zelia Lor. Not Quigox. Not Nalos. And definitely not Inquisitor Jeremias.'

'But he rescued us from the Orks. He saved us.'

'Only after firing on the *Profiteer*.'

'They shot first. We saw that.'

'We saw what Jeremias wanted
us to see. Do you really believe
Captain Amity would betray us? That
Flegan-Pala would betray us?'

'They abandoned us on Weald.'

Mekki turned back to the displays.
'Flegan-Pala went to protect the
Diadem. Captain Amity was injured.'

Zelia shook her head. 'I don't know
what to think. Jeremias seems pretty
convinced she's guilty. And then there's

all that stuff about the slaves...'

'The past can be manipulated,' Mekki said, before slamming his hand onto the input device in frustration. 'No!'

Zelia couldn't risk touching him again. 'What's wrong?'

'There is not enough power to contact the ship.'

'You're trying to contact the *Profiteer*.'

Mekki twisted his haptic implants in the ports, opening and closing files quicker than Zelia could read them.

'I need to talk to Flegan-Pala,' he said. 'To hear what really happened.'

'If he tells you the truth...'

'I will know if he is lying,' Mekki insisted. He flicked a switch and a map of the metropolis appeared on the screen.

'What have you found?'

He pointed at a large building on the map. 'That is a vox-tower. It should have enough power to transmit a message to the *Profiteer*.'

'If they're in range.'

'They will be,' Mekki said. 'Flegan-Pala will be looking for me. He will be looking for us all. We need to warn him about Inquisitor Jeremias.'

'That he's trying to find them?'

Mekki nodded, pulling his implants clear of the ports.

'But what if Jeremias is right, Mekki? What if Amity and Fleapit have been conspiring against us?'

He turned to face her, his expression grave. 'You cannot trust an inquisitor.'

'Even one that stopped you being arrested?'

'If he did, it was only because I serve a purpose. And when that purpose is fulfilled...'

He left the sentence hanging.

Zelia shook her head. 'I don't know, Mekki. We've been under a lot of pressure. It's no wonder you're feeling paranoid.'

'It is not paranoia,' he insisted. 'I know inquisitors of old.'

Zelia's pulse quickened. 'You mean...?'

He nodded. 'From before your mother took me in, yes.'

This was it, Zelia thought. Mekki was finally going to tell her what had happened to him all those years ago. He was going to tell her why he left Mars.

'Mekki, what Quigox said... about the Cult...'

The Martian glanced at Grimm. 'Not here. But I will explain, I promise.'

'On the way to the vox-tower?'

'You will come with me then?'

'Come on,' she said, creeping over to the front door. If they did this, not only would they be leaving Talen behind, they'd also be crossing an inquisitor. Either would be bad, but Mekki was her friend, and he needed her.

Grimm never even noticed them leave.

CHAPTER SEVEN

Second Attempt

'Are you ready?' Nalos inquired from behind his controls.

'Are we?' Talen asked Jeremias, who nodded. The inquisitor was trying to look confident, but Talen had already noticed the way he gripped the chair. He was nervous, maybe even scared.

And all the time Grimm barked through the locked door.

'Doesn't that thing ever shut up?' Talen asked.

'Not if it senses danger.'

'Danger to you?'

The inquisitor shook his head. 'Not exactly.' He held out his palm. 'The lume-compass, if you will.'

Talen passed the star to Jeremias and the inquisitor wrapped his fingers around the bloodied points, his body arching in the chair. The cables connected to the helmet pulsed, brighter than before. Talen shielded his eyes, the same terrible pressure already building in his head. His vision blurred, the sound of Jeremias's screaming distorting, merging with the incessant bark of the cyber-hound outside.

Wait – *Jeremias* was screaming? Talen tried to focus on the inquisitor but was having difficulty concentrating. It felt like hot needles were being plunged into his brain. He couldn't imagine what it was doing to Jeremias.

The inquisitor's body started to shake uncontrollably. He was having some kind of seizure. Nalos pressed a button and restraints snapped around Jeremias's arms and legs, holding him in position.

'What are you doing?' Talen shouted

at the tech-adept. 'You're killing him!'

'I concur,' Corlak burbled. 'Disconnect the Cognis.'

'No!' Jeremias gasped. 'I can almost see them. I can see Amity and her pet. They are near.'

Talen sank to his knees, clutching his head. 'The pressure,' he sobbed. 'It's too much!'

'The power must be stabilised,' Nalos said, connecting three of his mechadendrites directly into the terminal. 'I will make contact with the psychic boosters, use my own neural pathways to regulate the fluctuations.'

'Negative,' Corlak snapped. 'The risk is too great.'

'A risk to me?' Nalos asked. 'Or your master?'

'Both! Without you, he may perish in the attempt.'

'Let him continue,' Jeremias bellowed, the muscles in his neck standing out like ropes. 'I almost have their location!'

Nalos threw a switch and energy

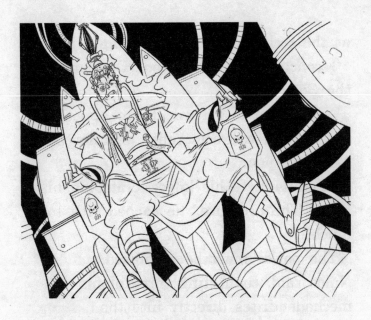

surged along his mechadendrites into
the cluster of cybernetic implants on
his crooked back.

Talen staggered back, still grasping
his head. In the chair, Jeremias started
to babble, a strange guttural language
that sounded more like someone
choking than speaking. If they didn't
stop soon, they would burn out the
inquisitor's mind, marooning Talen and
the others with no way off the planet.

He forced himself towards the control
terminal, reaching for the tech-adept,

who convulsed where he stood.

'Need to stop...' Talen gasped. 'You're going to kill him... You're going to kill us all.'

He grabbed Nalos's robes, spinning the tech-adept around. The adept teetered unsteadily on his cybernetic feet, his hood falling back.

Talen felt the gorge rise in his throat. Nalos's pale skin had turned green, pulsating boils spreading virulently from the tech-adept's implants. The breathing apparatus fell away to reveal a drooling mouth, its tongue purple and swollen, blackened teeth jutting from receding gums like gravestones.

Nalos grabbed Talen's vest with mottled hands and pulled him close, his breath rancid as he wheezed a strangled plea:

'Help me... please...'

CHAPTER EIGHT

Mekki's Story

Zelia was struggling to breathe, even with the oxygen mask strapped tight across her mouth. The streets of Aparitus were like an oven. Every doorway they passed added to the discomfort, heat pouring out from the volcano furnaces that burned at the heart of every manufactorum. Then there was the noise: the constant grinding of gears, the hiss of pistons and the relentless strike of hammers against metal. How the Adeptus Mechanicus worked in these conditions was beyond her, especially in all those robes.

But work they did. Zelia doubted Aparitus was ever quiet, with the production lines running continually, night and day.

Not that she could see the imposing bastions of industry that belched out fumes she could taste even through the rebreather. The city was drenched in a thick, ochre fog. It was impossible to see where you were going, and Zelia kept having to jump out of the way of servitors lugging heavy equipment, or adepts scuttling from building to building on metal legs. Skimmers and transporters whizzed overhead, the smog swirling in their wake. They'd only travelled a few blocks, but Zelia was already totally

disorientated, having to rely on Mekki and the map he'd downloaded before they left the workshop.

'How much further?' she asked, her voice muffled by the mask.

The Martian checked the display of his wrist-cogitator. 'Not far at all.'

'That's great,' she lied, leaning against a wall. The metal was painfully hot, but she needed to rest. 'Just let me catch my breath, okay?'

'We do not have time,' Mekki insisted, peering into the brume.

'Just calm down,' she told him. 'No one's following us. Not that they'd be able to in all this fog.'

He tapped the screen impatiently.

'Very well. But we cannot wait long.'

'Thanks.' She had another reason for wanting to stop – her curiosity. 'So... about this Cult...'

He frowned at her. 'You wish to discuss that now?'

She shrugged. 'As I said, I need a breather.'

He looked around again, and then moved in close, lowering his voice so she had to strain to hear.

'Back on Mars, my parents belonged to a faction...'

'The Cult...'

'A *faction* who believed that standard template constructs were limiting human development.'

'And what are they?'

'What are what?'

'The standard template whatever-you-just-said?'

'Standard template constructs,' Mekki repeated. 'They are a record, an index containing the sum total of human knowledge.'

'So far, you mean?'

He shook his head. 'Not according to the Mechanicus. The STCs contain the blueprints for every building, every weapon, every vehicle and every tool utilised by the Imperium. There can be no deviation. That's why the hives of Targian look so similar, for example, to the hives of Aralan or Regallus.'

'Because they're constructed using the same plans.'

'And built with exactly the same tools.'

'So, your parents thought they could do better?'

'They thought they should be allowed to *try*. The Adeptus Mechanicus are narrow-minded at best and fanatical at worst. We are not allowed to innovate, to think for ourselves.' He lifted the exo-frame that encased his withered arm, the servos creaking. 'According to the STC, this limb should have been removed at birth, replaced with a bionic device...'

'But you followed a different path.'

A tech-adept swept past, robes billowing. Mekki grabbed Zelia, pulling her into the shadows until he could be sure they hadn't been overheard.

'I knew we could save my arm,' he whispered. 'I built this with my mother. That was a happy day.' He looked at her, tears welling in his grey eyes. 'My parents always encouraged me to think beyond the STC. I have been inventing all my life.'

Zelia frowned. 'But if innovation is prohibited...'

'The faction was betrayed. They were reported to the Inquisition.'

'And that's why you don't trust Jeremias.'

He nodded. 'We were dragged through the streets. Sent for processing.'

She frowned, confused. 'What kind of processing?'

Mekki cocked his head, indicating the stomp of heavy servitor boots on the walkways.

Zelia's skin crawled as she realised

what he was saying. 'So, you mean...'

'All the stories about servitors are true. Some are grown in vats but the majority are those who dared to break the rules, to innovate...' His face darkened. 'To refuse to fight in the Imperium's wars.'

She felt sick. 'Like Talen.'

'We were determined not to suffer their fate,' Mekki continued. 'I fought my way out and have been running ever since.'

'What about your parents?'

A tear ran down the boy's cheek, cutting a path through the grime of the city. 'They sacrificed themselves so I could escape Mars.'

Zelia thought of the pain she felt being separated from her own mother. At least she knew her mum was alive. Mekki had never had that.

'You were alone.'

'At first, yes. I fell in with some... questionable individuals before I met your mother. She needed help on the

Scriptor so I invented the servo-sprites.'

Zelia smiled at the thought of Mekki's favourite inventions, tiny winged robots no larger than a strike-sparrow. She remembered the day her mum had showed them to her, how she'd laughed as they'd flitted around the *Scriptor*'s storage bay.

She wanted to pull Mekki into a hug, to tell him that it was all going to be all right, but she knew he wouldn't thank her. Instead she settled for two simple words: 'I'm sorry.'

Mekki looked down at his wrist-screen, pretending to study the map. 'We should be going.'

'Yes,' she agreed, tightening the straps of her mask. 'We should.'

He surprised her as he took her wrist, leading her through the fog. She flinched, not from his touch but as something sharp stung her cheek. 'Ow?'

It was like being jabbed by an invisible needle. She wiped her face, her fingers coming back wet. She shook the water from her fingertips. That hurt!

She went to look up.

'No,' Mekki said, stopping her. 'It's started to rain.'

She felt the colour drain from her already sore cheeks. 'Acid rain?'

Mekki checked the auspex in his wrist-screen. 'Not potent enough to cause serious damage, but if it becomes heavier...'

She grabbed his hand. 'Which way to the tower?'

They walked for ten minutes. The rain was clearing the fog, but was also becoming heavier by the minute. Zelia's face already felt as if it had been scrubbed with an iron brush and the fabric of her jacket was steaming in the downpour.

'Here we are,' Mekki said, shielding his eyes so he could look up at the tower that rose majestically in front of them like a gigantic spire. Pipes clung to its sloping sides, fans the size of voidship turbines whirring behind the sigil of the Adeptus Mechanicus, a cybernetic skull surrounded by a sharp-toothed cog.

'The vox-transmitter is on top of that?' Zelia asked, her jacket over her head to protect her face from the stinging rain.

'Indeed it is, although the real question is how we are going to get up there.' He glanced at the entrance to the building, which was guarded by armed skitarii. 'I doubt they are going to let us wander in.'

Zelia pulled her omniscope from beneath her jacket, snapping open the telescopic lens to search the spire's riveted walls.

'There's a landing platform,' she said. 'Ten. Maybe twelve storeys up...'

'My question still stands, unless you have learned how to fly?'

Zelia ignored the question as a low-flying grav-truck forced them to duck, the blast of its stabilisers churning up the rubbish on the streets before it. Mekki noticed her smiling as she watched the traffic weaving through the crowded skies.

'Zelia Lor?'

She beamed at him from behind her mask. 'Mekki, I have an idea, but I'm not sure you're going to like it...'

CHAPTER NINE

Infection

'Stay back!' Talen shouted as Nalos lunged for him. The tech-adept's pleas had soon deteriorated into wordless groans, his cracked lips curled into a bestial snarl.

Only his mechadendrites held him back, their tips still jammed into the cogitator terminal, which was smothered in rust. None of this made sense. One minute Nalos had been fine, the next he was covered in oozing blisters, his swollen features twisted in murderous rage.

'Do not let him touch you,' instructed Corlak, who was trying to release the unconscious inquisitor from his restraints.

'I wasn't about to!' Talen snapped, looking for a weapon to defend himself while Grimm clawed against the door. 'Perhaps we should let in your pet?'

'Negative,' Corlak said. 'The master forbade it.'

'Your master is comatose!'

Sparks burst from the console as the putrid tech-adept ripped himself free. He lurched forward, servo-arms grasping for Talen.

'Oh, I've had enough of this,' Talen said, leaping for the door controls.

Grimm didn't even wait for the door to open fully, scrambling through the widening gap to throw himself at Nalos, metal teeth already tearing at the adept's robotic tentacles. Talen didn't want to watch – he'd already seen what the mastiff could do to its prey. He ran to Jeremias, swatting away Corlak's fronds as he tried to help free the inquisitor.

'Is he breathing?'

'Barely,' the servo-skull replied. 'You open the cuffs around his wrists. I shall release his feet.'

Talen strained against the metal, feeling it give beneath his fingers. He gritted his teeth and tried not to listen to the sounds of tearing metal and snapping jaws behind them. The first cuff cracked open, but the second proved more stubborn.

'Haven't you a tool for this?' he asked, standing aside to let Corlak prise the metal apart with its pincers. With Grimm and Nalos still fighting behind him, Talen reached for the helmet.

'No!' the servo-skull shouted, trying to snatch his hands away. 'Don't! The shock will be too great.'

But Talen had already ripped the helmet from Jeremias's head. The inquisitor's eyes snapped open. His freed hand closed around Talen's neck, his fingers squeezing tight.

'What did you do?' he hissed. 'What did you do?!'

'What did *I* do?' Talen repeated, pulling himself free. 'What about *him*?'

Jeremias turned to see the tech-adept pinned down by Grimm, blistered hands holding back the hound's mechanical head.

'No...' he breathed as he took in the diseased skin. 'The Plague Lord...'

'Who?'

Jeremias scrambled from the chair, Corlak only just releasing the last cuff in time. The inquisitor grabbed Talen, bundling him towards the door.

'We need to get out of here.'

'You think?'

'But, sire,' Corlak began, only to be cut off by his master.

'Grimm will deal with the corrupted. Move.'

They ran into the workshop, only stopping at the sound of tearing metal. They whirled around to see Grimm suspended over Nalos's misshapen head by the tech-adept's rusting mechadendrites. With a choked howl, Nalos tore the robotic beast in two, sparks raining down on the floor followed by both halves of the crudely bisected body. The cyber-mastiff's limbs jerked, claws skittering uselessly on the ground, before lying still, the red glow of its once fearsome eyes fading until dark.

The tech-adept broke into a shambling run, making straight for them, corroded pincers snapping. Jeremias was transfixed, staring at his destroyed defender in disbelief. Talen pushed him aside, slamming the door controls. The door slid shut, separating them from the deranged tech-adept. Talen pressed every button he could find, looking for the lock, until Corlak reached across and flicked a switch.

'The door is locked,' the servo-skull reported as if nothing had happened.

'Can he open it from the inside?' Talen asked.

'I doubt he has the intelligence.'

'You're willing to take that chance?'

With an electronic sigh, the drone pressed a sequence of buttons. 'There. Happy now?'

'Not really.' Talen turned to Jeremias. 'What happened to him?'

But the inquisitor wasn't listening. 'Where are the others?' he wheezed.

Talen turned around. He had a point. Zelia and Mekki were gone.

'Maybe they went out into the corridor to search for scrying devices like you said?'

Jeremias lurched over to the exit to peer out into the gloom. 'There's no sign of them.'

Corlak floated over to the cogitator terminal Mekki had been using and accessed the log. 'They made no attempt to search for surveillance devices.'

Talen joined the servo-skull by the screen. 'Then what were they doing?'

'The Martian child attempted to send a message in binaric.'

Jeremias staggered up to them, supporting himself on a cluttered workbench. 'Send it where?'

'Into the void.'

'Perhaps they were trying to contact Zelia's mum,' Talen suggested. 'We've been looking for her ever since Targian.'

Jeremias didn't look convinced. 'Translate the message.'

The servo-skull accessed the transmission and read back Mekki's words in its usual stilted tones. 'Flegan-Pala. Come in Flegan-Pala. This is Mekki.'

Talen couldn't believe his ears. 'He was trying to contact the *Profiteer*?'

'Your friends have betrayed us,' Jeremias spat, as the trapped tech-adept banged against the door. 'They must be trying to warn Amity.'

'Warn her about what?'

'That we know what she's doing.'

'But we don't,' Talen spluttered. 'We don't even know she's behind all this.'

Jeremias grabbed him by the arms, staring deep into Talen's eyes. 'Really? Don't we? Search your heart, Talen. You know it's true. She tricked you. She tricked you all.'

Talen tried to pull himself away. Even if he was beginning to believe the inquisitor's words, he couldn't believe that Mekki and Zelia had turned against them, not after everything they'd been through together.

The inquisitor's grip on his shoulders eased and, with it, the edge in his voice. 'I know this is difficult, but you must at least face the possibility that your friends were in on it from the start.'

Talen shook his head defiantly. 'No. You saw Zelia. She was as shocked as I was when you told us the truth about Amity.'

Jeremias's hands fell away, but he didn't break his gaze. 'How well do you actually know them, Talen? The daughter of an explorator, who does

what? Dig up forbidden technology
from the dark times? And as for the
Martian – we've already heard that he's
a cultist... a heretic no less.' He looked
away. 'Perhaps I was wrong to protect
him.'

Talen's head was spinning. Had he
been duped? Had their friendship been
a lie all along?

In the next room, Nalos continued
banging on the door, patches of rust
appearing wherever his fists made
contact. Talen broke from Jeremias's
grip and railed against the sound.

'Shut up!' he yelled. 'Shut up! Shut
up! Shut up!'

He felt a hand on his shoulder, the
inquisitor softly saying his name.

'Talen...'

Wiping his eyes, he turned to Corlak.
'Did Mekki leave any clues where they
were heading? The space port maybe?'

The servo-skull glanced at Jeremias,
who nodded his permission. Cogs
whirred in the familiar's head as it

searched the log.

'Yes. The Martian accessed a map of the surrounding area.'

Jeremias straightened. 'That sounds promising. Any locations in particular?'

A grid appeared on the screen, a section of the map Mekki had been using. Talen studied it. 'How far is this?'

'A few blocks,' Corlak replied. 'Not far at all.'

Jeremias straightened his coat. 'Are you armed, Talen?'

'What? No. I had some bolas but they were destroyed back on Weald.'

The inquisitor rifled through the accumulated junk of a nearby workbench and, finding a power-wrench, handed it to Talen. 'This will have to do for now. Tuck it into your belt. Corlak will watch over you.'

The servo-skull swivelled from the screen, its mechadendrites realigning to reveal a beamer.

'As you command, sire.'

Jeremias pulled a rebreather from beneath his jacket and fixed it over his mouth.

'We're going outside?' Talen asked. 'Why not use the teleporter?'

'We cannot be sure if that's where they're heading,' Jeremias admitted. 'We're going to have to track them.'

Talen grinned. Now *that* was something he could do.

He wasn't feeling so eager when they got down to street level. It was raining, the water hissing as it hit the floor.

Jeremias removed his coat and threw it over Talen's shoulders, telling him to cover his head.

'What about you?' Talen asked.

'Your need is greater than mine,' the inquisitor insisted, turning up his collar and plunging into the rain. Within minutes, the man's shirt was steaming.

But that wasn't the worst of it. Following Corlak's directions they turned a corner to find themselves face to face with a tech-adept. Like Nalos, its mottled skin was blistered, its mouth full of blackened teeth. How had the disease spread so quickly? The revenant lurched towards them, swollen hands grasping for Talen's throat.

A sword whistled through the air. The tech-adept wailed as its severed hands dropped to the floor. With another swipe of his sword, Jeremias sent the diseased Mechanicus adept crashing to the ground to join them.

'Move,' Jeremias shouted, guiding Talen through the downpour. Corlak bobbed ahead, its bone-white skull sizzling before it suddenly stopped. More infected adepts were shambling towards them, arms outstretched.

Talen turned to see even more behind. They were all the same. The same murderous expression. The same blistered skin. The same rotting flesh.

The sickness was spreading.

It had become a plague.

CHAPTER TEN

Zelia's Plan

'Okay. You see those grav-carts?'

Zelia pointed out a group of servitors delivering parts to a nearby forge, the mindless drones oblivious to the stinging rain.

'Yes?' Mekki nodded, sheltering beneath a sizzling arch.

'Well, remember how you boosted our flyer back on Targian?'

'To escape the Necron scarabs.'

'Exactly. You – I don't know – supercharged the anti-grav generators to fire us into the sky.'

Mekki's eyes sparkled as he realised where she was going with this. 'You wish me to do it again, with one of those carts.'

She nodded, clutching her omniscope in both hands. 'Can you?'

'It is a crazy idea, Zelia Lor... but yes... yes, I can.'

'Then we'd better steal one,' she said, grinning wickedly.

They sneaked across the road, narrowly avoiding a speeding transporter. The driver yelled abuse as Mekki pulled Zelia back, but the servitors didn't look up, consumed by the task they'd been ordered to complete.

Zelia tried not to think about the drones' origins as they grabbed an empty cart and dragged it back to the vox-tower, grinning like wolf-cats. Step one of the heist of the millennium had been completed without a hitch... almost.

'Hey, what are you doing?'

That wasn't the grunt of a servitor. Zelia turned to see a hooded serf hurrying through the drizzle, an acid-proof data-slate in hand.

She jumped onto the grav-cart, the slab bucking beneath her weight. 'It's now or never.'

The Martian was on his hands and knees beside her, his haptic implants thrust into the inner workings of the hover-sled.

'Get off that thing,' the serf snapped, steam rising from her protective clothing.

'Mekki…' Zelia hissed.

'Almost there,' the Martian replied.

'Almost isn't good enough.'

The serf was upon them now, a hand already on the cart's handle. 'I said, get off.'

'We just need to borrow it,' Zelia said, trying to buy Mekki time.

The serf frowned. 'Borrow it for what?'

'This!' Mekki exclaimed, activating the anti-grav.

The cart shot up into the air, the serf still clinging to the handle. The slab lurched under the weight of three passengers, but righted itself as the shocked serf let go, tumbling back to the ground with a cry.

Zelia winced at the soft crump of the serf hitting the walkway and hoped that she wasn't too hurt, but for now had to concentrate on their own safety. She grabbed the handle to stop herself being thrown from the cart. Mekki was still on his hands and knees, fingers jabbed into the stabiliser control as they shot up the side of the towering spire.

'How high do we have to go?' he asked.

Keeping hold, Zelia glanced up at the loading platform she'd spotted earlier. 'About five or six storeys.'

The cart shuddered.

'Will it get us all the way up there?'

Mekki checked the access panel. 'The suspensors are burning out.'

She looked up. A maglev train was speeding past the tower, just below the platform. 'We haven't far to go.'

'Attempting to maintain power,' Mekki told her – or maybe even himself – as he fiddled with the suspension field.

They sped up, Zelia whooping with nerves and adrenaline. The cart shot past the train but flipped over in mid-air, the suspensors finally overloading.

Zelia and Mekki cried out as they tumbled from the slab to land on the speeding train. Zelia scrabbled for a handhold as she rolled perilously close

to the edge. Her fingers closed around a handle and she jolted to a halt, her legs dangling over the side. She pulled herself back onto the top, looking up to see Mekki trying to get to his feet on the next carriage. He'd made it too. He was safe.

For now, at least.

The train wasn't slowing. Soon it would be past the tower, continuing on its way to Throne-knew-where. She broke into a run, leaping to the next carriage, not stopping as Mekki joined her in racing towards the back of the train. She had no idea what they were going to do when they reached the platform. Launch themselves at the building? The landing pad was still above their heads and the rain was coming down harder than ever, stinging their skin as they tried not to slip.

Mekki shouted something, but she couldn't hear him above the thundering engine. She followed his gaze to see an open-top flyer shooting up from the streets below. If it stayed on its trajectory it would rocket up past them, and – more importantly – past the landing pad.

Was Mekki *seriously* suggesting they leap from a speeding train to land on a near-vertical air-skimmer? That was almost as crazy as riding a power-boosted grav-cart up the side of a tower, probably more so. Still, he was racing towards the edge, his tattered robes heavy with acid rain. Fumbling the omniscope back into her bandolier she matched the Martian step for step. She was trusting him on this. Mekki's mind rivalled any cogitator. If anyone could calculate the jump it would be him... she hoped.

The flyer climbed, the train thundered forward and the children ran, swerving towards the edge of the carriage at the last moment.

Zelia didn't know if she screamed as she leapt into the air, her arms pinwheeling, but she definitely cried out as they landed with a thud in the back of the skimmer. The pod shuddered, and the driver glanced back to see what had hit him. His eyes widened when he saw two children in his hold, Mekki hanging over the edge of the grav-car to check their position.

'We are over the platform,' he shouted, just as the driver banked hard. Zelia tried to grab hold of the seat as she was pitched out of the flyer. She plummeted down, throwing out an arm as she dropped past the landing pad. She jolted to a halt, dangling in mid-air. Mekki had grabbed the rail on the edge of the platform, his good arm taking the strain, exo-frame creaking as he held onto her with his other hand. Sparks were already flying from the frame's creaking servos.

'Climb up me,' he hissed through clenched teeth and she nodded, using the frame to pull herself up. Mekki's entire body was shaking as she reached the rail, swinging her leg onto the

platform. She rolled onto the pad,
twisting around to grab Mekki before
his arm gave way. Crying out with the
effort, she yanked him over the edge.

They lay on their backs, breathing
heavily in their masks, bodies aching
and minds spinning. If either of them
had fallen...

No. They couldn't think like that. Not
now. Not with caustic rain drenching
their already raw skin.

Mekki struggled up, his weak arm
hanging uselessly at his side. The frame
wasn't working, the servos jammed. He
limped over to the doors but couldn't
raise his haptic implants to the access
point. Zelia did it for him, the frame's
metal joints squeaking as she lifted his
arm.

'A little higher,' he said, before his
fingers found the connectors and his
electoos flashed. The door slid open and
they tumbled into a thankfully empty
loading bay.

Zelia dropped to her knees as the

door crashed down behind them again. She pushed the rebreather aside, gulping in the tower's recycled air.

She looked up at Mekki, who shook his head at her, before starting to laugh. She joined in and before long they were almost hysterical, clutching their sides, their laughs echoing around the deserted bay. Zelia had never heard Mekki laugh so long and so hard. It was a good sound.

But they had to keep moving. There was no telling when someone might walk into the storage bay, or a skimmer might land on the platform outside. She forced herself to breathe deeply. Mekki had sat up, tears streaming down his scalded face. He probed the exo-frame, his arm still hanging lifelessly.

'Can you fix it?' Zelia said, wiping her eye and wincing. Her skin felt like it was on fire, her clothes full of holes.

He shook his head. 'Not here, but it should not be difficult with the right tools.'

She helped him up. 'Like the tools on the *Profiteer*?'

He nodded, walking cautiously to double doors that led to a maze of corridors. 'First of all we need to find the transmitter array.'

'Or a cogitator connected to it.'

He flashed her a smile. 'Now you are starting to think like me, Zelia Lor.'

'I'll take that as a compliment,' she said, activating the controls.

The doors slid open.

CHAPTER ELEVEN

Indestructible

Talen and Jeremias were surrounded. The ganger brandished the wrench, wishing that he had something that could do more damage.

Plague zombies were everywhere. Zelia would roll her eyes at the name, but she wasn't here, was she? She wasn't the one ringed by a mob of swaying, moaning monstrosities in a city overrun by shambling horrors. Everywhere he looked he saw faces distorted by the same disease that had ravaged Nalos, their skin the colour of mouldy cheese and their features twisted by bulging blisters. He had trusted Zelia and she had left him in this nightmare. Jeremias was right. She *had* betrayed him, and just when he needed her most.

The nearest zombie lurched towards Jeremias and Talen swung the power-wrench, knocking a malfunctioning servo-arm out of the way. The mechadendrite sparked, its gears whirring. Whatever ailment was mutating the adepts was also affecting their cybernetics, foul-smelling goo dripping from every joint and coupling.

'Why is this happening?' Talen asked, but the inquisitor countered with a question of his own.

'Where is Corlak?'

Jeremias was the reason they hadn't got far. He had to keep stopping, leaning against corroded walls to stay on his feet. Talen had gone to return his coat, but the inquisitor had insisted that he keep it over his head, even though the inquisitor's clothes were now frayed and his skin raw.

'I need to protect you,' he'd wheezed, gripping the hilt of his sword in both hands. Talen wished that the inquisitor had given him the blade. It would be more effective than a tool.

Talen looked around, but there was no sign of the servo-skull. He wondered if the zombies had got hold of Corlak, and the macabre assistant was lying in pieces in some back alley, ripped apart by malfunctioning mechadendrites. If they could destroy something as formidable as a cyber-mastiff, a solitary drone wouldn't stand a chance.

'Corlak...' Talen shouted, jabbing at a groaning serf with a grotesquely distended neck. 'We could do with a hand here. Or a pincer. Or whatever you have at the end of your arms.'

Something brushed his back. He swivelled around, lashing out with the wrench, knocking a diseased hand away. The plague zombie hissed at him through splintered teeth.

The mob pressed in, spurring Jeremias

into action. The inquisitor slashed with his sword, slicing down two... no, three of the ailing attackers. Three more fell, not to the singing blade but to sudden bolts of las-fire. Jeremias had drawn his beamer and was twisting and firing, some shots going wide, while most found their targets. He was magnificent, even in his weakened state, although the strain of the fight soon proved too much. The inquisitor stumbled, his beamer slipping from his hand. It slid across the walkway to be trampled beneath zombie feet, the las-bursts having attracted even more revenants.

'Give me the sword,' Talen demanded, but Jeremias shook his head.

'No. Only an inquisitor may wield Purifier.'

Talen swiped at a zombie with the wrench, the rain stinging his wrist. 'Well, it's either that or we get ripped apart. Your choice.'

Jeremias wasn't listening. He was on his knees, staring into the rain. 'Need to be strong,' he muttered, wide-eyed and exhausted. 'Need to fight the contagion.'

Talen pivoted on his heel, looking for escape routes. He could probably make a break for it, but Jeremias could barely stand, let alone run.

It was useless. The zombies closed in and Talen turned to the inquisitor, ready to wrestle Purifier from his hands. Inquisitor or not, he had to do something.

Or did he? The sudden roar of an engine drowned out the zombie horde and Talen looked up to see a covered skimmer cutting a swathe through their attackers. It screeched to a halt beside them, its door swinging up to reveal Corlak at the controls.

'Get the master on board!' the servo-skull ordered and Talen did as he was told. He bundled the inquisitor into the grav-car, yelling at Corlak to go. The servo-skull obliged, gunning the engines before the door had even closed. They shot into the air, a zombie throwing itself onto the bonnet as they climbed into the rain. There was no way of knowing if the creature had been an adept or a serf. All Talen knew was that it was punching the windscreen, desperate to get in.

'Do not fear,' Corlak said, as Talen draped the coat that had protected him over Jeremias's shoulders. 'That is reinforced armourglass – all but indestructible.'

'Someone needs to tell him that,' Talen said, as the zombie continued its single-minded assault. 'Where did you get this thing anyway?'

'I commandeered it from a nearby street.'

'Stole it, you mean.'

'Its owner was no longer capable of piloting a vehicle.'

'They'd become one of those things?'

'The infection is spreading, yes.'

'But how?'

Outside, the zombie produced a bionic

arm that ended in a whirring saw. Sparks sizzled in the rain as the teeth ground into the reinforced glass.

'Now is not the time for conversation,' Corlak said.

'For once I agree with you,' Talen said, screwing his face up at the sound from the saw. 'We need to get it off us!'

'Agreed,' the servo-skull said, slamming the flyer into a sharp roll. The zombie hung on, as cracks spiderwebbed from the saw's spinning teeth.

'I think I'm going to be sick,' Talen groaned, hanging onto the pilot's seat.

'Not on me, you're not,' Jeremias snapped.

'Back with us then?' Talen said. 'Any idea how to dislodge a stubborn zombie?'

'Yes,' the inquisitor hissed. 'Corlak, electrify the window.'

'What?' Talen exclaimed. 'We're in a metal box. Won't we be electrified too?'

'Says the boy who can handle shock-sticks. Corlak – do it now!'

The servo-skull stabbed an electro-prod

into the window frame and electricity
crackled around the armourglass,
sweeping over the zombie's body. It held
on, arms rigid, blue sparks dancing
around its clenched teeth.

'It's persistent,' Talen said. 'I'll give it
that.'

As they watched, the pustules on the
zombie's face swelled, its entire body
bulging as if it was about to burst –
which it did with a sickening squelch,
exploding into a seething mass of tiny
green creatures. They slapped against
the armourglass, little balls of slime
with snarling mouths, malevolent eyes
and long, pointed horns.

'What are they?' Talen gasped.

Jeremias stared at the creatures
with a mixture of hatred and fear.
'Nurglings,' he
snarled as if
the name was
explanation enough.

The cackling
imps hung onto

the windscreen, stuck fast by the disgusting slime that covered their equally disgusting bodies. They scratched at the glass, their tiny claws as hard as diamond.

Talen could feel hysterical laughter bubbling up from his stomach. Earlier today, he would have happily told you that zombies weren't real and now had watched an electrified revenant explode into a swarm of giggling horrors. He was being flown through the air by a cybernetic skull while monsters bayed for his blood on the streets below.

Nothing about this made sense, but there was one thing he was certain of – he wouldn't be in this mess if Zelia and Mekki hadn't left him behind.

CHAPTER TWELVE

The Transmitter

Nothing could have prepared Zelia for the temperature inside the tower. The air was stifling, every surface hot to the touch. She could only imagine the size of the furnace in the base of the spire, the heat from it rising up the structure like smoke up a chimney.

Mekki had found a number of terminals, but none of them could access the transmitter. He had at least found schematics of the building, locating a cogitator hub four floors up. He had led the way, finding a spiral staircase which would take them up to the right floor, only for them to nearly run into a team of maintenance-serfs, grumbling as they fixed a faulty lifter.

Zelia had pulled Mekki into a doorway, willing the bondsmen to complete their duty. As they stood there, shoulder to shoulder, she thought about what Mekki had told her, scolding herself for not asking about his parents before today. Not that he would have answered. Mekki had always been secretive, holed up in his cabin on board the *Scriptor* with his gadgets and gizmos. They had lived in each other's company for years and known so little about each other. Zelia vowed that they would never fall back into their old ways if they ever made it home. They would be closer, maybe even more like brother and sister. She was the only family Mekki had left.

Finally, the serfs finished their task and headed off, their hover-trolley squealing.

'Sounds like a faulty motivator,' Mekki muttered, and Zelia had a terrible suspicion that he was going to leap from their hiding place to offer his services. But the Martian stayed where he was, and the workers left.

Zelia breathed out a sigh of relief.

'How much further?' she asked, wiping sweat from her stinging eyes.

'This way,' he said, leading her to a large door. He pressed a control and it slid open to reveal a room full of terminals.

'Is this it?' she asked as Mekki locked the door behind them before crossing to the main cogitator. 'Need me to help?' she added, nodding at the access points.

'Please,' he said, allowing her to lift his bad arm so his implants could reach the ports.

Nothing happened.

Usually, needle-thin connectors slid from Mekki's fingertips to plug into whatever system he was trying to access, but this time the implants remained dormant.

'The damage must be worse than I

thought,' he said, pulling up a seat. As she watched, he started flicking switches, the screens coming to life in front of them. 'I will have to do this manually.'

'But you can still activate the transmitter?'

He didn't reply, the fingers of his good hand a blur as he typed.

Zelia took the opportunity to look around, breathing a silent 'wow' as she spotted the panoramic window that dominated the left-hand wall.

The city stretched out in front of her, a sea of chimneys belching noxious fumes into the atmosphere. She took a few steps forwards, imagining millions of workers toiling away in the heat of the vaulted manufactoria. The fruits of their labour would be sent all across the Imperium, from tanks and weaponry to starships and farming equipment. Maybe some of the tools in her mother's workshop back on the *Scriptor* even originated here, just one of thousands of similar planets dotted through the galaxy.

Suddenly, Zelia felt very, very small.

Behind her, Mekki called out in triumph.

'Have you done it?' she asked, rushing back to him. 'Have you accessed the transmitter?'

'Yes,' he said, flicking a series of switches. 'I am boosting the power, as I did on Hinterland Outpost.'

'When you nearly fried a Tau warship!' she reminded him.

Something approaching pride flickered across the Martian's face. 'That was a focused burst. This should merely extend the transmission as far as possible. If I know Flegan-Pala, he is already searching for us.'

A nagging doubt picked away at the back of her mind. 'Unless...'

He looked at her, his good humour evaporating. 'Unless Jeremias was telling the truth. Unless he really is working with Captain Amity.'

Zelia nodded. She hadn't wanted to say the words out loud.

Mekki shook his head. 'I cannot believe that. I will not. But, just in case the captain *is* listening, I am attempting to contact Flegan-Pala on a frequency of his own devising.'

Binaric symbols scrolled up the screens.

'Is this how you usually communicate?' Zelia asked, watching the seemingly endless stream of ones and zeroes.

Mekki nodded, glancing down at Zelia's sleeve as her vox crackled. She did the same, noticing a flashing light beneath the speaker grille. Before Mekki could stop her, she flicked the switch and a familiar voice buzzed over the open channel.

'Zelia? Zelia, please come in.'

'Talen?'

'There you are! We've been looking for you everywhere. Why was your vox not working?'

Mekki looked away, obviously

embarrassed. She thought back to him grabbing her arm as they trudged through the fog. Had he deactivated it so they couldn't be contacted?

'I'm with Mekki,' she said, cocking a suspicious eyebrow at the embarrassed Martian.

'Where?'

'At the vo–'

Mekki shot out a hand, cutting the communication.

'Mekki! What's wrong with you?'

The Martian looked at her defiantly. 'We cannot trust Talen Stormweaver.'

'Of course we can!'

'Not when he is with the inquisitor.'

She sighed, shaking her head. 'Look, I understand why you're wary of Jeremias, but Talen's our friend.'

'Can we be sure?' he asked.

'She cut me off,' Talen complained as his vox-box went dead.

'And you're surprised?' Jeremias asked as the skimmer swerved to the right,

dislodging more Nurglings from the
windscreen. The disgusting creatures
were now trying to squeeze in through
the cracks around the doors, their vile
bodies compacting like balls of pus as
the flyer rusted before Talen's eyes.
Holes had already appeared in the roof,
and corrosive water was starting to
drip through.

At least the windscreen seemed to be
holding, despite the persistence of the
Nurglings that had yet to be thrown
clear by Corlak's increasingly erratic
flying.

'Can't you zap them again?' Talen
asked the servo-skull.

'It wouldn't do any good,' Jeremias
rasped. 'They are creatures of Chaos.'

'You keep saying things like that as
if I should know what you're talking
about,' Talen said, trying the vox-box
again. It was no good. There was no
way to raise Zelia.

Unless...

He turned to Corlak. 'When we were

on Weald, we found Mekki by tracking his vox-signal. Can you trace Zelia's last-known location using my vox?'

'Of course I can,' Corlak replied testily, a tentacle snaking out to grab the battered box from his hand. 'Here, take the controls.'

'I am ready,' Mekki said, as the cogitator bleeped.

'You've boosted the signal?'

The Martian nodded. 'Flegan-Pala will hear us, as long as the *Profiteer* is in range.'

'And what is the range?'

Mekki checked the equipment one last time. 'Oh, three to four star systems.'

Her mouth dropped open. 'Three to four? Is that even possible?'

Mekki grinned. 'It was not, until I got my hands on it.'

Almost immediately a light flashed on the vox set deep into the console, but fists banged on the door before Mekki could even reach for it.

'Open up in there!'

The children wheeled around. They didn't recognise the muffled voice, but there was no mistaking the urgency of the knocking.

'You will open this door at once!'

Mekki swivelled back to the vox, flicking a switch. 'Flegan-Pala, this is Mekki. Please respond.'

Behind them, the door erupted in a blaze of blue light. Zelia threw up her arms to protect her eyes from the glare as boots tramped into the room.

'Did you think you could hide from me, renegade?' Quigox gloated as she swept through the ruined door. 'This time, there's no one to protect you.'

CHAPTER THIRTEEN

Pop Goes the Nurgling

'Tell me what you were doing with the transmitter,' Quigox demanded as the skitarii stood guard, their weapons trained on the children.

'I refuse,' Mekki said, trying not to whimper as one of the adept's tentacles whipped towards him, the pincers grabbing his face.

'I admire your spirit, but I will learn your secret, even if I have to slice the information from your brain.' As if to illustrate her point, she produced another mechadendrite, this one tipped with a buzzing laser-scalpel.

'We were trying to contact Fleapit,'

Zelia blurted out as the device snaked towards Mekki.

Quigox frowned at the name.
'An unlikely alias. What is he? An abhuman?'

'He's a Jokaero.'

'A weaponsmith?' Quigox's silver eyes gleamed. 'Imagine the knowledge such a being could bestow. Where is this "Fleapit"? Out in the void?'

When neither child responded, Quigox brought the laser dangerously close to Mekki's cheek. He stammered an answer in binaric, which seemed to please the adept.

'On a spaceship,' she translated. 'Searching for you... Then he must find you.'

'I don't understand,' Zelia said. 'You want him to come here?'

'Of course,' Quigox told her, as if the answer was painfully obvious. 'Knowledge is power, and thanks to your beast, I will be the most powerful adept on the planet.'

On board the skimmer, a Nurgling had almost squeezed through a jagged hole in the door. Jeremias kicked out, shoving it back through the gap. The Nurgling screeched as it was snatched away by the wind, another immediately taking its place.

'How much further?' the inquisitor growled, wiping the sole of his boot on the floor.

'The girl's signal originated on the thirteenth floor of that vox-tower,' Corlak dutifully replied, pointing towards a tall spire on the horizon.

Talen brought the skimmer around. 'Just above that loading platform?'

Jeremias peered over the boy's shoulder. 'Yes. That is where we must land.'

'Yeah, about that...' Talen said as they rocketed ahead. He was trying to pull back on the throttle, but the flyer wasn't responding.

Jeremias cursed beneath his breath. 'The Nurglings must have chewed through the air brakes.'

'We are going to crash!' Corlak squawked.

Talen's grip tightened around the flight stick. 'Which floor did you say she was on?'

'I will not betray Flegan-Pala,' Mekki said, trying to pull away from the laser.

Quigox dragged him towards the terminal. 'You will do what I say,' she commanded, grabbing his withered hand and thrusting his fingers towards the access points.

'His implants aren't working,' Zelia cried out.

The adept glared angrily at her. 'More lies.'

'It is the truth,' Mekki insisted. 'The connectors are damaged.'

But Quigox wasn't listening. She was staring at the panoramic window, her mouth open. A skimmer was flying straight for the tower, small creatures swarming all over it.

'Run!' Zelia shouted, gambling that the skitarii wouldn't shoot.

They didn't have a chance. With an ear-splitting crash, the flyer smashed through the window. It slammed into the floor, skidding across the room to smack into the far wall, demolishing a bank of cogitators.

'Mekki?' Zelia called out as the dust settled, turning to see dozens of tiny green goblins scuttling from the wrecked flyer.

The skitarii fired, picking off the

marauding imps with bolts of blue energy. The creatures shrieked as they were hit, bursting in a haze of sulphurous gas. The noise was almost comical – *POP POP POP* – but there was nothing funny about the smell.

The rusty door of the skimmer swung open and Jeremias dived out, sword in hand. 'Don't breathe in the fumes.'

'I wasn't about to,' she told him, pulling on her rebreather.

POP POP POP.

'Behind you!' Quigox shouted as more creatures spilled from the skimmer's corroded roof.

Jeremias spun on his heel, slicing through them with his blade – *POP POP POP* – before Corlak swept out of the vehicle to help evaporate the others.

POP POP POP POP.

When the room was finally clear, Jeremias pointed his sword at the adept. 'What is the meaning of this, Quigox?' he demanded.

The adept looked at him as if he

were mad. 'You crash in through
a window, your craft infested with
Throne-knows-what. I could ask you the
same question!'

'And yet, interrogation is my speciality,
not yours.'

'Tell that to her drill,' Zelia muttered
to herself.

Jeremias viewed her with barely
disguised disgust. 'You have something
to say, traitor?'

She scrambled up, glass crunching
beneath her boots. 'Traitor? We were
just trying to...' Her words fell away.

'Trying to what?' Jeremias asked.

'Just trying to contact Amity,' Talen
said, glaring at Zelia as he clambered
from the skimmer. 'How could you?'

'How could I?' Zelia wasn't having
that. 'Talen, what evidence do we have
that she betrayed us?'

'Jeremias told us.'

'And you believe him?'

'Why shouldn't I? He's an inquisitor.'

'And you're a ganger,' she pointed

out. 'Since when have you listened to authority?'

'Since he realised that the Imperium will protect him,' Jeremias snapped. 'A lesson you would do well to remember.' The inquisitor glowered at Mekki. 'You and your cultist friend.'

Zelia took a step forward. 'But it wasn't a cult. Mekki's family just wanted to–'

'Silence!' Jeremias bellowed, although Zelia couldn't help but notice that he swayed slightly as he turned to Quigox. 'You will release the boy into my custody.'

'He is my prisoner,' the adept insisted.

'And he will be returned to you once our mission is completed.'

'You said you were protecting him,' Zelia said, going to put herself between Mekki and the inquisitor. Talen rushed over to stop her.

'Zelia, stop,' he said, grabbing her arms. 'You need to listen for once. Something terrible is happening. We need to trust Jeremias.'

'What?' Quigox asked, her curiosity piqued. 'What is happening?'

'We haven't time for this now,' Jeremias snapped.

'Haven't time? Inquisitor, I demand an explanation.'

Jeremias stepped towards the adept, ignoring the arc rifles that tracked him across the room. 'You're not in a position to demand anything! Your planet is facing certain doom, but I can request urgent assistance from the Imperium.'

Quigox looked as though she was about to argue, before grudgingly releasing Mekki. 'What must we do?'

'We must return to Nalos's workshop,' Jeremias told them. 'We will be safe there.'

'Are you sure about that?' Talen asked. 'Last time we were there, Nalos tried to kill us.'

'He did what?' Zelia asked.

'This time we will have skitarii to

protect us,' the inquisitor said, glancing at the tech-adept. 'Is that not right, Quigox?'

'It seems I have very little choice,' she said, glowering at Jeremias.

'Then we are agreed,' the inquisitor said, looking at the wrecked skimmer. 'Although we may have to secure new transport.'

'There is a storage bay on the lowest level,' Quigox told him. 'We can take a transporter.'

'Excellent.' He turned to leave, but Talen stopped him.

'Wait. Before we go, how was Mekki trying to warn Amity? Did he contact the *Profiteer*?'

'No,' Quigox said. 'He said he was contacting a Jokaero.'

'Fleapit!'

'Talen, please...' Jeremias warned him. 'We are running out of time.'

'No, you don't get it. We should let him make contact.'

Zelia went to grab him. 'Talen, what

are you saying?'

He shrugged her off. 'Amity doesn't know we're with the inquisitor. She has no idea we know the truth about her.'

Jeremias was studying him intently. 'Go on...'

'We should vox them, tell them that we've found a planet brimming with artefacts, treasures just like the Diadem.'

The inquisitor considered this. 'She'd come running.'

'Bringing the Diadem with her.'

'And we'll be waiting.'

'No,' Mekki said. 'I will not betray Flegan-Pala, whatever you say.'

'Maybe you don't have to,' Quigox said, turning to study the data on the cogitator screens. 'The transmitter is locked into a frequency I have not seen before.'

'A direct line to the xenos?' the inquisitor asked.

Quigox turned to him. 'If I do this, you will request help for my planet.

The Adeptus Astartes?'

Jeremias nodded and the adept jabbed a mechadendrite tip into the access point, the metal tentacle clicking as it established a connection. Quigox spoke, but not in her own voice. It was a perfect imitation of Mekki, even down to his precise enunciation.

'Fleapit, this is Mekki. Can you hear me? Fleapit, come in!'

'Clever trick,' Talen said, as Quigox lied about finding a hidden stash of xenotech.

Zelia whispered in the ganger's ear. 'Talen, this is wrong. You know it is.'

'Wrong?' he said, turning on her. 'I'll tell you what's wrong. The streets down there are swarming with zombies.'

'What do you mean?'

'Exactly how it sounds. Nalos attacked us, reducing Grimm to scrap. And then we were mobbed in the street. We need Jeremias to get us off this junk heap and he won't leave until he has the Diadem.'

'So you're going to trick Amity?'

'She tricked us first.'

'And what makes you think you can trust him?' Zelia said, shooting a dark look at the inquisitor. 'We don't know him, Talen.'

'We barely know each other! But he gets me. He... he listens to me.'

'And what? You're going to become his apprentice?'

Talen shrugged. 'Is that such a crazy idea?'

'So much for never wanting to fight!'

'I didn't want to become a soldier, but Jeremias is different. Besides, the fight keeps finding me anyway. Perhaps it's time I took the hint.'

At the terminal, Quigox finished her message.

Jeremias peered at the screen. 'Have you made contact?'

The adept didn't answer.

The inquisitor repeated the question, irritation creeping into his voice. In response, the adept let out a low, keening groan.

Zelia felt Talen stiffen beside her. 'Oh no. Not again.'

'What is it? What's wrong?'

'That!' Talen replied as Quigox reeled around, boils erupting all over her face.

CHAPTER FOURTEEN

Escape

'Stay back!' the skitarii commander rasped, as Quigox lurched forward, her skin darkening to a mottled green. The guard opened fire and the adept was sent flying back into the cogitators, her body erupting into a pack of snickering Nurglings.

'Everybody out,' Jeremias barked as the skitarii picked off the putrid pests, Corlak joining in the fight. Zelia didn't run at first. She was rooted to the spot, watching in horror as the creatures swarmed over the skitarii commander. He tried to brush them off, but they wriggled through gaps in his armour, mouldy teeth snapping.

Mekki grabbed Zelia, pulling her towards the exit, Talen running alongside. They turned when they were safely over the threshold. The commander was convulsing where he stood, green sludge seeping between the joints of his armour. And then he raised his weapon and fired, the blast almost hitting Corlak.

'He's been infected!' Jeremias shouted, ducking as another shot zapped over his head. 'Destroy him!'

The skitarii turned on their commander, their blue bolts hitting him square in the chest. The guard's body ruptured beneath his armour, and another wave of Nurglings spilled out. Talen yelled a warning as they scampered up the inquisitor's coat, but it was too late. A Nurgling sank its teeth into his shoulder. Jeremias didn't even scream, but slammed his back against the wall, the Nurglings popping on impact.

There was a scream as the second skitarius succumbed to the sniggering creatures.

'Retreat,' Jeremias commanded, squashing Nurglings beneath his boots as he raced for the door. The last skitarius hesitated before turning his rifle on his comrade and putting the howling guard out of his misery. The armour clattered to the floor, disgorging even more slime-bags.

'Run!' Jeremias bellowed as he and the remaining skitarius barrelled out of the wrecked room. The children didn't need any encouragement. They tore down the corridor, a tsunami of Nurglings washing after them.

'How are there so many of them?' Zelia asked.

'Trust me, that's the least of our worries,' Talen replied as he ran a few steps ahead. 'The entire planet is swarming with those things and no one seems to know why.' They reached a junction, the corridor branching into two. 'Which way do we go?'

'Down here,' Mekki told him, holding his weak arm as they raced towards the lifter doors. Talen thumbed the buttons and the doors opened, the children scrambling in as Corlak and the skitarius attempted to keep the Nurglings at bay.

'Come on!' Talen said as the skitarius waited for the last moment before backing into the waiting lift, arc rifle blazing.

The doors closed, squishing at least three Nurglings who were trying to follow him through.

'Do you think they will follow us down?' Mekki asked.

There was a thud from above, followed by another and another.

'Does that answer your question?' Talen asked as the telltale scratching started up again above their heads.

'What is your designation, skitarius?' Jeremias asked the guard.

'Kraxx-Eighty-Seven, sir,' came the response.

'Interesting name,' Talen commented.

The guard's goggles swung around to face him. 'I was the eighty-seventh member of my batch.'

'Your what?'

'Skitarii are mass-produced,' Mekki explained, staring up at the rusty scratch marks on the ceiling. 'Constructed, not born.'

'Of course they are,' said Talen. 'Well, I'm sorry about your friends.'

'They died in service,' came the cold reply.

'They were infected,' Jeremias said. 'There's a difference.'

'Talking of which,' Talen asked, looking pointedly at the inquisitor's shoulder.

Jeremias glared at him. 'It is nothing.'

'You were bitten!'

Jeremias checked his beamer's powercell. 'My coat contains leech-spheres.'

'I don't know what they are,' Talen admitted.

'Tiny orbs that absorb harmful energies,' Eighty-Seven responded, peering curiously at Jeremias. 'They are sewn into skitarii robes. I wasn't aware that the Inquisition also utilised them.'

'We choose not to broadcast our secrets,' Jeremias said, fixing the skitarius with a commanding stare. 'You will come with us, Kraxx-Eighty-Seven. We need your protection.'

The guard nodded.

'Where are we going?' Zelia asked.

'Back to Nalos's chambers,' the inquisitor replied. 'We will wait there until Amity responds.'

'What about Nalos?' Talen asked.

'We have a skitarius,' Jeremias told him. 'And I am feeling stronger by the minute. We will be able to deal with a single zombie.'

'If we can even make it to his workshop. It's madness out there, remember.'

With a ping, the doors opened on a bay filled with armoured vehicles. Zelia braced herself, but no Nurglings came running. They were too busy trying to chew through the ceiling.

'Everyone out,' Jeremias commanded, leading them towards a bulky transporter. It was no battle tank, but it looked robust enough. It was also locked, but Corlak made short work of the bolts and the doors slid open, revealing benches across the armoured walls.

Behind them, Nurglings poured out of the lifter.

'They don't give up, do they?' Talen

said, leaping into the vehicle.

'Neither do we,' Jeremias said, herding the children on board as Eighty-Seven picked off the scampering horrors before jumping in through the door. The inquisitor slammed it shut as Talen clambered behind the steering wheel, much to Corlak's disgust.

'I will drive the vehicle,' the servo-skull insisted.

'Not this time,' Talen said, looking for the ignition.

Mekki leant over and pressed a big red button, the engine rumbling into life.

'You sure you can handle this thing?' Zelia said, sitting on the bench and strapping on a harness.

'There's only one way to find out,' Talen said, slamming down on the accelerator.

CHAPTER FIFTEEN

Lord of Decay

The transporter smashed through the bay-doors and onto the street, the wheels screeching on the road.

'Which way's the workshop?' Talen said, skidding to avoid a cluster of rampaging zombies.

'Straight ahead, then take the corner,' Mekki told him, barely glancing from the door, which was already rusting from the scrape of Nurgling claws.

'You helping us now, Mekki?'

'I do not wish to be infected,' Mekki replied matter-of-factly. 'Although the disease also seems to spread through the Mechanicus's *technology*. If I had been connected to the cogitator–'

'You would have turned into one of those things?' Zelia asked, gripping her chair as Talen swerved around the corner.

'That's what happened to Nalos,' the ganger told them, swinging the transport from left to right. 'He only became sick after he plugged himself into the control panel.'

'But why is it happening?' Zelia asked, clutching her harness as Talen veered to avoid hitting a diseased servitor.

'It is a plague,' Jeremias growled, 'a blight that has swept from planet to planet.'

'And what about those creatures?' Mekki asked.

'The Nurglings spread the contagion, infecting all they touch.'

'Unless you're protected by leech-spheres,' Zelia pointed out.

'Yeah – where can we get some of those?' Talen asked, the transporter shuddering as it lurched to the left.

'Not that they helped those skitarii back there.'

'Yes, I wondered about that,' Zelia said, holding on as Talen sent them screaming into another turn. 'Why weren't they protected?'

'Maybe their equipment was faulty,' Jeremias told her.

'Unlikely,' Eighty-Seven intoned.

'Either way, you're safe with me,' the inquisitor vowed.

'And Aparitus?' Eighty-Seven asked.

'Little can be done once the plague has a planet in its grip,' Corlak informed him.

'That is... unsatisfactory,' the skitarius replied.

Jeremias sighed. 'I will call for reinforcements.'

'You mean Space Marines?' Zelia asked, thinking of the armoured giants they had seen on Targian.

Jeremias nodded. 'Aparitus is a valuable resource. The Throne will not want to see it fall to the disease.'

'That isn't a guarantee,' Zelia pointed out, remembering what had happened on the hive world.

'For good reason,' Jeremias snapped. 'I am but one inquisitor, on a very specific mission. I cannot save everyone.'

Zelia shook her head. 'All you care about is the Diadem.'

Jeremias glared at her. 'You have no idea how many worlds would perish if the Diadem's true power was unleashed, how many lives would be lost. These are the kinds of choices I have to make every day. The fate of one planet against thousands. It's imperative that we recover the device. Nothing is more imp—'

His words were lost as something slammed into the side of the transporter. Talen fought with the steering wheel, but couldn't stop the vehicle from tipping over. It rolled, throwing them against their harnesses, until it skidded to a juddering halt.

'Is everyone all right?' Zelia asked,

hanging from her harness. The transporter was on its roof, the cracked windscreen hissing in the rain.

'Barely,' Talen said. 'What hit us?'

A huge mechanical leg smashed down in front of them.

'Does that give you any clues?' Zelia said, releasing her buckle to drop down beside him.

'Actually no,' he replied, staring up at the giant robotic figure that towered over them. It was armoured from head to toe, phosphor-blasters where its hands should be and a combustor-cannon mounted on its back.

Mekki scrambled over to see. 'It's a Kastelan robot. A war machine.'

'What?!' Jeremias exclaimed, joining them to stare through the window.

'At least it looks as if it's seen better days,' Zelia said, as it raised one of its arms, rusted plates clattering to the ground with every movement. That didn't stop it slamming its blaster down like a bludgeon. It burst through

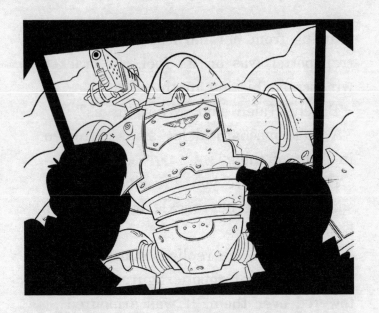

the bottom of the transporter, nearly spearing Jeremias. The transport shook as it pulled its arm free, ready to deal another blow.

The next time they might not be so lucky.

CHAPTER SIXTEEN

Old Friends

'Get back against the walls!' Jeremias yelled as the corroded colossus prepared to punch down, its hydraulic joints creaking.

'I will protect you,' Eighty-Seven shouted, positioning himself beneath the jagged hole the Kastelan had created, arc rifle aiming at the robot's armoured head.

'No. Fall back,' the inquisitor bellowed. 'That's an order.'

The skitarius prepared his shot.

'It's infected. Its defences may not be operational.'

'There's no way of knowing that.'

The enormous arm swung down.

Zelia screwed up her eyes as las-fire rang out, but it wasn't from the skitarius's beamer. Instead, bolts of energy were bouncing off the Kastelan's already dilapidated chassis. It jerked beneath the onslaught, shrapnel flying everywhere, before collapsing in front of the upended transport. Nurglings gushed from the fallen armour, but this time no one was looking at the imps. They were watching silhouettes traipsing towards them through the rain. There were three of them: one looking vaguely human, energy blasts streaming from a heavy-beamer, while a taller figure thwacked plague zombies with hammer-like hands. The third was taller still, lasers blazing from thick arms.

'Who are they?' Zelia asked before she became aware of shining balls of light that were zipping through the air, snatching up Nurglings or popping them with needles of pure energy.

Eighty-Seven went to fire as one of the mysterious orbs dropped through the hole the Kastelan had made.

'No!' Mekki shouted, pushing the skitarius's arm aside. 'It is not a threat!'

Zelia grinned as she recognised the gleaming automaton that flitted around the ruined vehicle.

'Meshwing! Is that you?'

The servo-sprite bobbed in response to its name.

'One of your creations?' Jeremias sniffed, as if ready to cleave the automaton in two.

Mekki nodded proudly. 'Originally, yes. Although, by the looks of things she is not alone.'

The door was pushed aside by a flock of the winged constructs, while others zapped zombies and Nurglings alike with laser-stings that streamed from their delicate fingertips.

A figure appeared in the doorway, tall and elegant with a rebreather clamped

to her face, but there was no mistaking the sweeping green coat or the tricorne hat that steamed in the acid rain.

'Amity,' Jeremias hissed.

'At your service,' the rogue trader replied, twisting to blast a plague zombie who'd got past the servo-sprites.

'Hand over the Diadem,' Jeremias demanded, brandishing Purifier.

Her eyebrows shot up. 'You want to do this now? I don't know if you've noticed, but this planet is swarming with... well, I don't exactly know what they are, but they smell awful and seem intent on killing anything that moves, so let's save the ultimatums for when we're safe, yes?' She looked around the wrecked transport. 'You do have somewhere safe, don't you?'

An infected adept loomed up behind Amity before anyone could answer her question. Zelia called out a warning and Amity ducked as a bolt from Eighty-Seven's rifle reduced the zombie to a pile of snarling Nurglings.

'Ugh! What are these things?' Amity said as a swarm of servo-sprites descended on the imps. 'Actually, don't answer that. Just get moving, okay?'

For once, Jeremias didn't argue. He leapt from the transport, the children scrambling after him. Zelia heard Talen gasp and turned to see what he was gaping at.

'Is that...?' he asked, and Zelia grinned from ear to ear.

'Yes. Yes, it is.'

A Tau battlesuit stomped towards

them, not as bulky as the Kastelan, but the very same armour they had stolen from Hinterland Outpost. It was picking off zombies, a familiar pilot working the controls behind a transparent bubble that sat where its chest-plate used to be.

'Flegan-Pala!' Mekki shouted happily.

'Save the reunion for later,' Jeremias said, pointing across the street. Talen had got them back to Nalos's building after all, its front door hanging from its hinges. They ran through the battlefield, Fleapit taking out any zombie that lurched too near while Corlak and Eighty-Seven joined the servo-sprites in the fight against the Nurglings.

As Zelia ran for the door, a plague zombie grabbed her bandolier. It yanked her back and she screamed, expecting the clammy touch of diseased fingers around her mouth at any moment. It never came. With a sickening crack, the monster was sent flying through the air, limbs flailing. Zelia twisted around to see Grunt, the servitor's hands replaced with bulky warhammers, weapons the drone put to good use by knocking another zombie off its blistered feet.

Talen pulled her back towards the door. 'Zelia, come on.'

She let herself be dragged over the threshold, standing aside as Grunt thundered after her.

'What about Fleapit?' she asked as Jeremias went to barricade the door. The inquisitor stopped as the Tau battlesuit stomped over to the building, the transparent bubble sliding aside to allow Fleapit to jump down. The shaggy alien grunted at the suit, which turned to protect the doorway, blasting any zombie that came near.

'You automated it,' Mekki said, obviously impressed. The Jokaero responded by snatching up the door, pushing it back into place, fixing the hinges and then, when it was safely locked, wrapping Mekki in a hairy hug.

For once, the Martian didn't mind,

although the inquisitor looked as if he was going to be sick.

'Everyone upstairs,' Jeremias said, nose turned up as he regarded the Jokaero.

Amity pulled the rebreather from her face. 'Lead the way.'

Jeremias shook his head, his knuckles white around the hilt of his sword. 'You first. I want you exactly where I can see you.'

Amity rolled her eyes. 'Didn't I just save your life?'

'Oh, we haven't got time for this,' Zelia said, shoving past them to run up the stairs. 'Come on.'

CHAPTER SEVENTEEN

The Diadem

'Wait,' Talen said as Zelia went to open the door to Nalos's chambers. 'He's one of those things, remember.'

'The skitarius will go first,' Jeremias said, standing aside so the armoured guard could stalk past.

They followed Eighty-Seven into the workshop. The place was as they'd left it, although the internal door was pitted with dents. Eighty-Seven inched forward, rifle raised as Jeremias, Amity and Corlak fell in behind, weapons drawn. A swarm of servo-sprites hovered above, fingers splayed and ready to rain down las-stings on anything that moved. The children kept back, Meshwing perched on Mekki's shoulder, and Fleapit stayed close to Grunt.

Jeremias glanced at Mekki. 'You. Open the door.'

The Martian crept to the controls and pressed a sequence of buttons. The door slid partially aside, jamming in the frame.

The chamber beyond was dark, the candles long since guttered. There was no movement, except for the dust motes swirling in the stale air. No one spoke and no one moved.

Finally, Jeremias took a step forward, sword raised.

With a gargled roar, Nalos burst from the darkened room, scuttling on his mechanical arms like a wolf-spider. At least, they assumed it was Nalos. His head was unrecognisable, a misshapen growth, pitted with the rusty remains of his cybernetic implants, his swollen limbs hanging from a hideously bloated body.

Eighty-Seven didn't wait for a command. He opened fire and Nalos exploded into the now-expected gush of Nurglings. Zelia stepped back, banging into Fleapit as the servo-sprites went to work, blasting the vile creatures from every conceivable angle.

One of the imps darted forward, beady eyes fixed on Zelia before it was popped by Meshwing. Zelia's skin crawled. The little horned beasts reminded her of something, but try as she might she couldn't remember what it was.

Amity cried out as a Nurgling scuttled up her back. The captain spun around, trying to dislodge the creature.

'Blast it,' Jeremias yelled at Eighty-Seven, not caring that Amity would be hit too.

The skitarius pulled his trigger, the beam slicing through the air towards Amity. Grunt lurched forward, throwing himself in front of his captain. The blast slammed the servitor into Amity, sending her beamer skidding across the floor as they landed in a heap, the Nurgling popped beneath their combined weight.

'What did you do?' Amity said, hauling Grunt onto his back. The servitor was out cold.

'It's just a drone,' the inquisitor snapped, sword drawn. 'It can be repaired.'

Amity sprung back to her feet, drawing her own cutlass. She lunged, their blades clashing as the inquisitor expertly blocked the attack.

'I assume our partnership is at an end,' Amity said, as Jeremias thrust forward.

'It never began.'

The rogue trader parried, feinting to the left before freezing as she saw her own beamer pointed in her direction.

Amity stared at the gun. 'Talen? What are you doing?'

'You need to give him the Diadem,' the ganger said, staring down the sights.

'What?'

'It's over, Amity. We know who you really are. Jeremias showed us. He told us what you did.'

The captain glared at the inquisitor. 'Did he now?'

'Give him the Diadem!' Talen shouted.

'I haven't got it!' she yelled back. 'Fleapit has it locked away in that inter-dimensional portal thing on his back.'

Corlak swept towards the Jokaero. 'You will surrender the artefact to me.'

Fleapit bared his teeth at the servo-skull.

'I do not think he is going to,' Mekki said, smirking at the drone.

'Yes,' Zelia said softly. 'Yes, he is.'

Mekki looked at her as if she'd gone mad. 'Zelia Lor?'

Zelia raised her hands in surrender. 'I'm sorry, Mekki, really I am, but I've had enough.'

'Enough of what?'

'Enough of all the running, and the arguing, and the monsters and the betrayal. And for what? An alien artefact we know is dangerous.'

'But you promised you would take it to your mother. You promised you would take it to Elise Lor.'

'Yes, I did. But look around us, Mekki. We have a plague spreading like wildfire, zombies beating down the doors and we're pointing guns at each other. No promise is worth all that. I know you don't like the Inquisition, and I understand why, really I do, but

they know what to do with this stuff.
Jeremias deals with these things every
single day. We're just kids, Mekki.'

'You do not mean that.'

'Don't I? Look at the chaos we've
caused, all the people who have died.'

'You're making a mistake,' Amity
warned.

'That's all we've been doing,' she told
her sadly. 'One mistake after another.
It's time we stopped.'

Zelia turned to Fleapit. 'Please. Give
him the Diadem. It's over.'

Scowling, Fleapit flexed his shoulders
and, with a clunk, the dimensional pack
opened. He reached inside and produced
the Diadem, the pack snapping shut
once more.

'At last...' Jeremias exclaimed,
snatching the artefact from Fleapit's
hands. 'After all this time.' He stood for
a moment, running his fingers across
the strange glyphs on the metal crown.
Then he straightened, forcing himself to
look at Zelia. 'You chose wisely today,

my dear. Now will you help me?' He
looked around the room. 'Will you all
help me?'

'What choice do we have?' Mekki
muttered.

'You could fight?' Amity said, glaring
at the inquisitor.

Jeremias ignored her, turning to
Eighty-Seven. 'You will guard the
prisoner. She must not interfere.'

'Interfere with what, my lord?' the
skitarius asked.

'You asked if I would help your

planet? With this I can,' the inquisitor replied, holding up the artefact. 'As for you,' he continued, turning to Fleapit. 'Can you be trusted, xenos?'

'Yes, he can,' Mekki insisted. 'And his name is Flegan-Pala.'

'Then let him prove himself.' Jeremias pointed at the servo-sprites. 'Take these... things and see how that battlesuit of yours is faring. If we're going to do this, we need to be free from distractions.'

'If we're going to do what?' Talen asked as Fleapit reluctantly lolloped back out into the corridor, the servo-sprites streaming after him. Only Meshwing stayed with them, crouched on Mekki's shoulder.

Jeremias approached Talen and held out a hand. 'First you give me that. I need your hands free.'

Talen did as he was told and the inquisitor slipped the beamer into his belt. Then the colour drained from his face and he stumbled. Both Zelia and

Talen jumped forward to help him.

'Are you quite all right, sire?' Corlak asked, his mechadendrites twitching in concern.

Jeremias waved them away, still gripping the Diadem. 'I am fine.'

'Is it the bite?' Talen asked.

The inquisitor wiped hair from his eyes. 'Merely the effects of being near the Cognis device, but all is well. In fact, we will use the psychic amplifier to cure the infection.'

'How?'

'Just do as I say,' Jeremias growled. 'Please.'

He staggered into the darkened chamber, and the children made to follow him.

'No,' Jeremias said, raising a hand to stop them. 'You must wait outside, just for a moment, until we check that it is safe. Corlak?'

The servo-skull swept into the room to check the control panel.

'Some of the circuitry has corroded,' it

reported. 'But the equipment seems to be operational.'

'But what about the plague?' Zelia reminded him. 'If you use the technology…'

'It's a risk I'm willing to take,' Jeremias rasped, indicating for Talen to join him. The ganger stepped eagerly through the door, which immediately slammed shut. He spun around, shocked.

'Did you mean to shut them out?'

'Yes,' Jeremias said as Corlak grabbed Talen's wrists with its pincers. 'Nothing must be allowed to interfere with the preparations.'

'Preparations?' Talen grunted as he was dragged towards the Cognis chair. 'What preparations? What are you doing? Let go of me!'

Corlak shoved him into the chair and the restraints snapped around his wrists and ankles, holding him in place. Talen struggled but there was no way to break free.

Jeremias staggered towards him, the Diadem in his hands. He twisted the artefact and it separated into two identical rings.

'I didn't know it did that,' Talen said, wriggling as the inquisitor tried to place one of the rings over his head.

'Oh, there's much about the Diadem you don't know,' Jeremias said as he lowered the Necron crown onto Talen's brow.

CHAPTER EIGHTEEN

The Truth

'Open up! Open up!'

Zelia hammered on the door, while Mekki and Meshwing attempted to see if they could override the lock.

'Stop that,' growled Eighty-Seven, still holding Amity at gunpoint.

'I told you it was a mistake trusting him,' the rogue trader said.

'And I should have believed you,' Zelia said, running at the skitarius. The guard turned as Zelia slammed into him, trying to yank the arc rifle from his grip. He pulled the weapon free, his armoured elbow catching her in the face. She went down, head throbbing, as

Amity attacked, throwing herself at the armoured warrior. He stumbled, but was too strong, and pushed the rogue trader back. Still dazed, Zelia scrambled to her feet as Eighty-Seven brought his rifle up and–

CRACK!

The guard clattered to the floor. In his place stood Grunt, hammer-hands raised in case Eighty-Seven still had fight in him, but the skitarius lay still.

'Good to have you back, Grunt,' Amity said, rubbing her neck as she used a table to pull herself back to her feet. 'Now knock down that door.'

Mekki stood aside as the lumbering giant stomped over to slam his hammers into the rusty metal.

'What are they doing in there?' Zelia asked.

'Maybe we can have a look,' Mekki said, hurrying to a screen. Meshwing went to plug her data-connectors into the cogitator, but the Martian stopped her.

'No. The infection is spreading through the technology, remember?'

'Should you be touching it, then?' Amity asked, looking over his shoulder.

Mekki found a terminal that was reasonably free of rust. 'I should be fine as long as I do not connect using my haptic implants. Infection only seems to occur when directly linked to the system.' He continued flicking switches with his good hand. 'If I can just get the internal pict-feeds working...'

An image of the Cognis chamber appeared on one of the screens. Zelia gasped as she saw Talen trapped in the central chair, a metal band pressed down on his head.

'Is that the Diadem?'

Mekki pressed more controls and the ganger's angry voice crackled over the vox.

'What are you doing? Let me go.'

'I'm afraid I cannot do that,' Jeremias said, slipping the second half of the

Diadem over his own head. It caught on the inquisitor's silver mask, and Jeremias winced as if in pain.

Corlak hovered to its master. 'The mask will have to be removed, sire, if the procedure is to be a success.'

'Procedure?' Talen asked, still struggling against his restraints. 'What are you planning to do to me?'

Talen fell silent as the inquisitor pulled off his mask to reveal puckered green skin. This wasn't the effect of the acid rain. The scars looked

old – Jeremias's cheek was covered in weeping sores.

'It's you,' Talen gasped. 'You're the source of the infection. You're the source of the plague.'

A look of sadness passed over Jeremias's mismatched face. 'Unfortunately, the use of the psychic amplifier must have passed my... condition into the technology of this planet.' He handed the mask to Corlak. 'The Mechanicus talk of machine-spirits that dwell in all cogitators. Perhaps those spirits can be corrupted as easily as flesh.'

He looked Talen straight in the eye. 'I didn't ask for this. I was infected long ago when fighting Chaos Space Marines on Feston. I felt the disease creep into my mind even as we brought them to their maggot-strewn knees. It's been in there ever since, squirming like a slime-snake, but I was strong. I've kept the plague at bay by any means possible while I searched for a cure

– rejuve treatments, arcane technology...
even sheer force of will.'

'That's why the Nurgling didn't affect
you,' Talen realised. 'It didn't have
anything to do with leech-spheres. You
were already infected. And I trusted
you. I *defended* you. What else have
you lied about? Amity and the slaves?
Was all that a pack of lies too?'

The boils on Jeremias's face pulsed.
'Your friend *was* disgraced...'

'Because she sold a flotilla into
slavery...'

'Because she *freed* a consignment
of slaves she was paid to transport,'
Jeremias snapped. 'There, that's
the truth. Are you happy now? The
slaves belonged to Molinda Kolbrun,
a particularly corrupt governor in the
Taramus Sector.'

'So he revoked her commission to
cover his tracks. And you knew all
along.'

'Of course I knew,' Jeremias snarled.
'And what difference did it make? She's

a rogue trader, a nobody, but me...?' He leant forward, so close that Talen could smell the rot on his breath. 'I'm an inquisitor. Have you any idea what it is like to suffer this indignity, this shame?' He tapped his head with a shaking finger. 'Every day I feel the infection getting stronger, but I have my duty. I can't fall. I won't. The Diadem is my last chance, and by the Emperor's name, I mean to take it.'

Jeremias pushed himself up, teetering slightly. Free of the mask, the boils were spreading across his face, the infection finally taking hold. He staggered to the second chair, falling into the seat as the hammering on the door intensified.

'Hurry, Corlak,' he wheezed. 'We haven't long.'

The servo-skull flitted between them, using cables to link the two halves of the Diadem.

'But I still don't understand,' Talen admitted as the servo-skull completed its work. 'What have I got to do with this? You said we were going to work together.'

Jeremias giggled. It was a horrible wet laugh, more like a Nurgling than a man. 'And we will, Talen... just not as you expected. This is the Diadem of *Transference*, boy.'

'And what exactly does it transfer?'

'Minds,' the inquisitor replied, his lips beginning to crack. 'My mind will be free of this corrupted flesh.'

Talen's stomach lurched as he realised what Jeremias was saying. 'You're going to transfer into *me?*'

'You are strong. A little young maybe, but I'm running out of options.'

'But what about me? What will happen to my mind?'

'You will be trapped in the master's body,' Corlak told him. 'It is an honour.'

'An honour? Have you seen it?'

The infection was spreading rapidly now, Jeremias's once handsome features all but consumed by pulsating boils.

'Please,' said Talen, making one last attempt to break free. 'Don't do this.'

'It is my duty to survive,' Jeremias croaked, his lips swollen to twice their normal size. 'Not that you'd understand anything about duty, the boy who ran from the service of his Emperor. The boy who abandoned his post. Abandoned his family.'

'I thought you understood! You said we would do great things together.'

'And we will,' Jeremias crowed. 'That's the beauty of it. Together we shall continue the Emperor's work. We will serve... serve...' The rest of the sentence was lost as Jeremias was wracked by a coughing fit, his entire body convulsing.

'We must begin,' Corlak announced, sweeping to the controls. 'The master's mind must be saved.'

'No,' Talen cried out. 'Corlak, stop!'

But the servo-skull was already flicking switches. 'Your sacrifice will not be in vain, Talen Stormweaver. You will finally serve your Emperor.'

Corlak pulled one final lever and the ring around Talen's head blazed with light.

CHAPTER NINETEEN

All in the Mind

Talen's scream burst from the vox-speakers. Both halves of the Diadem were glowing, purple energy flowing between the two crowns.

'We have to get in there,' Zelia said, as Grunt continued to pummel the door.

'We will,' Amity said, ordering the servitor to move aside. The rogue trader had Eighty-Seven's arc rifle in hand, the sleek barrel pointing towards the door. She fired, bolts of electric blue reducing the rusty barricade to dust.

The captain strode into the Cognis chamber, aiming at Corlak.

'Shut it down!' she commanded as

Zelia and Mekki rushed to Talen. The Diadem had stopped glowing and the boy's head lolled awkwardly forward, his chin resting on his chest. The inquisitor was slumped in the other chair, hair falling out and eyes swollen shut.

'You are too late,' Corlak rejoiced. 'The procedure is complete.'

'No!' Zelia said, shaking Talen's shoulders. 'Talen, can you hear me?'

'Zelia?' he croaked, his voice little more than a whisper.

'Yes. Yes, it is me. Let's get you out of here.' She struggled with the restraints. 'Mekki, can you help me?'

The Martian hurried towards Corlak, who produced its own beamer.

'I wouldn't,' Amity warned, her finger tightening around the trigger.

The servo-skull floated aside and Mekki found the right control. The restraints snapped open and Talen tumbled forward, the Diadem still tight around his head. He sprawled across the floor, landing at Amity's feet.

'Is he all right?'

Zelia knelt beside him. 'You are, aren't you, Talen?'

He tried to turn over. 'I need to get up.'

'I'll help,' she said, hooking her hands beneath his arms. 'That's it.'

She got him to his feet. He leant on her, clutching his head.

'Talen?'

'I'll... I'll be all right in a moment... I just need... to think...'

'Think about what?'

BANG! BANG! BANG!

Zelia looked up. Something was hammering on the front door, the sluggish rhythm accompanied by a chorus of muffled groans.

'Plague zombies,' Amity hissed. 'They must have got past Fleapit. We need to get out of here.'

'We can use the teleporter,' Mekki said. 'Teleport ourselves back to the inquisitor's ship. If I can connect the console to the *Zealot's Heart*...'

'No, don't,' Zelia said. 'You'll infect our only means of escape.' She turned to Amity. 'Unless we can use the *Profiteer*?'

The rogue trader shook her head. 'If only. We only just made it to Aparitus. Your sick friend over there fired at us the moment he arrived on Weald. We didn't stand a chance, especially after the crash.'

'I said that the battle-footage was doctored!' Mekki said.

'Now isn't the time for told-you-sos,' Zelia said as rust started to spread across the outer door. 'Corlak, you need to teleport us to safety.'

'I only answer to the inquisitor,' the servo-skull said.

'Then answer to me now,' Talen said, throwing himself at Amity. The attack took everyone by surprise, especially the captain, who was slammed against the wall. Grunt raised a hammer to protect his mistress, but Talen turned on his heel, the arc rifle in his hands.

'I wouldn't, you senseless brute,' he

said, stepping back so he could cover all of them with the stolen weapon.

'Talen, what are you doing?' Zelia asked.

Talen brought the gun around to face her. 'Not Talen... Jeremias.'

'Sire?' Corlak asked, its tentacles quivering.

'The procedure was a success,' Talen announced, his voice noticeably lower than before. He sounded like Jeremias.

In the next room, the door opened a fraction, blistered fingers appearing through the crack.

Talen glanced into the workshop. 'They're breaking through. Corlak, prepare the teleport.'

The servo-skull bobbed smugly. 'Gladly, sire.'

'All of us.'

Suddenly Corlak didn't sound so sure. 'Including the heretics, master?'

Talen smirked. 'I think it's about time Captain Amity and her cronies were brought to justice. We'll send them to the work camps of Marell, the servitor included. They will see out their days making ammunition for the Imperial Guard.'

'You can't do that, Talen,' Zelia pleaded.

The boy sighed in annoyance. 'How many times have I got to tell you, girl? Your friend is trapped in that festering heap over there.' He nodded at the inquisitor's bloated body, still slumped in its restraints. 'The choice is yours. I leave you for the zombies, or deliver you to Marell. Which is it to be?'

Zelia fell silent. What choice was there?

'I thought so. Ready, Corlak?'

'Ready, sire.'

With a pitiful moan, the inquisitor's old body began to thrash in its chair.

The boy who used to be Talen smirked at the pathetic creature. 'Say goodbye to your friends. We're going on a journey, a very long journey. Now, Corlak.'

The teleport's hum filled the room as the outer door disintegrated under the weight of the plague zombies. They streamed into the workshop as the inquisitor's former body raged ineffectively in its chair.

Zelia closed her eyes as the nauseating energy of the teleporter washed over her, the buzz drowning out the groans of the infected horde and the dismay of the friend they were leaving behind.

When she opened them again, they were back on the *Zealot's Heart*.

'Excellent work, Corlak,' the servo-skull's master said as it swept towards the flight controls.

'Shall I set course for Marell, sire?'

'Actually,' he replied, lifting the arc rifle, 'I've changed my mind.'

The servo-skull exploded as it was hit by a bolt of crackling energy.

'There, that's better.'

Zelia stared at him, for once lost for

words. Had the inquisitor lost his mind?

He looked at her and grinned. 'What's the matter, Ladle-Girl? Don't tell me you fell for it, too?'

Ladle-Girl? But that's what Talen had called her when they first met...

'The procedure didn't work!' she gasped. 'You're still you!'

'Course I am,' Talen said, throwing the rifle back to Amity. 'Sorry about the shove back there. I had to make Corlak believe I was the real deal.'

'So it was all an act?' Mekki asked.

'A convincing one,' Amity said, shoving the rifle into Zelia's hands and making for the flight controls. 'This is some ship.' She slipped into the flight chair as if she belonged there, priming the engines with a flourish.

'Are we going somewhere?' Zelia asked, passing the gun to Grunt.

'Back to the workshop,' Amity told her, pulling back on the flight stick. 'The long way round.'

* * *

Once upon a time, Flegan-Pala would have enjoyed sitting in a Tau battlesuit, blasting zombies. He would have enjoyed blasting anything, to be honest.

But now... now, he was worried. Not about himself... but those foolish younglings. He hadn't been able to stop the zombies fighting their way into the building and was now pinned down by hundreds if not thousands of those Nurgling creatures desperate to break into the suit. To make matters worse, the suit's joints had rusted solid as it succumbed to the plague that blighted this world.

The servo-sprites were all gone, swatted from the air by Nurgle-controlled mechadendrites or ground beneath blistered feet.

He was alone. Just as he'd always been.

He mashed the triggers one last time. The pulse-cannon didn't respond. He tried again, but the guns were jammed.

There was only one thing for it.

Twisting open the control panel,
he pulled out a handful of wires.
The armour's power pack was still
operational. Perhaps he could convert it
into a bomb. He could jump clear and...
BOOM!

Flegan-Pala chuckled at the thought of
the explosion, but his simian features
fell as the powercell failed a second
later.

The armour toppled over, landing
face down. Claws scraped against the
bodywork, teeth crunching the corroded
metal.

There was no way out. He was
trapped.

Then, the roar of a voidship made
him smile, as did the percussive
rattle of las-fire. Zombies wailed and
Nurglings popped as Flegan-Pala's smile
became a toothy grin, teleportation
energy crackling across his fur...

'We have him,' Mekki cried out as
Fleapit materialised on the teleport pad.

'Then it's time to go,' Amity said, pointing the *Zealot's Heart* towards the sky. The inquisitor's ship streaked into the heavy clouds, leaving hundreds of zombies gnashing their rotten teeth far below.

Soon they were back among the stars. Amity turned to see Talen standing awkwardly behind her. She nodded at the co-pilot seat.

'Want to pick up where we left off?'

He rubbed his neck. 'I'm sorry.'

She frowned at him. 'What for?'

'For believing Jeremias's lies. About you.'

She smiled, winking at him. 'Nobody will blame you. I am pretty shady.'

Talen blushed just before Zelia threw her arms around him, catching him in a bear hug.

'Get off!' he laughed, pushing her away. 'What brought that on?'

'You saved us,' Zelia said. 'Thank the Throne the mind-swap didn't work.'

'The Throne had nothing to do with

it,' Mekki said, plucking the Diadem from Talen's head with his good hand. He peered at the artefact, a lens dropping down in front of his eye. 'As I thought. This is a fake.'

'A fake?' Zelia turned to look at Fleapit, who was smiling slyly. As they watched, the Jokaero opened his dimension pack and retrieved the real Diadem of Transference.

The alien grunted, Mekki translating for the rest of the group. 'Flegan-Pala created a duplicate. He guessed that

the inquisitor was after the Diadem, just as he guessed that it was not really me who sent the transmission.'

'How?' Talen asked, and in answer Mekki played back a recording of Quigox pretending to be him.

'Fleapit, this is Mekki. Can you hear me? Fleapit, come in!'

Talen still looked none the wiser.

'You need to listen more,' Zelia said, smiling as she saw his eyes widen.

'Mekki never calls him "Fleapit"!' he finally realised. 'How could I have been so stupid?'

'Do you really want me to answer that?' Mekki said, the ghost of a smile on his thin lips.

Talen grinned back at him. 'Watch it, Cog-Boy!' He looked around the austere flight deck. 'So what do we do now? Sure, we've got a new ship, but that doesn't help all those people down there.'

He was right. There was no telling how many Aparitians had fallen foul of the plague.

Amity sighed, staring at the planet below. 'There isn't much we can do, unfortunately. Once a plague has taken hold...'

'We can't just leave them,' Zelia said.

'And we can't fight a contagion of that magnitude.'

'We could tell someone about it,' Talen suggested. 'Ask for help.'

'We already have,' Mekki said from where he had been working controls, the Diadem resting on the console next to him. 'Or rather, the inquisitor has. I sent a distress call from his cogitator using his ident codes. The Space Marines will come.'

'And what happens when they don't find him waiting?'

Mekki shrugged. 'They will think he succumbed to the plague, which is true. At least this way, they might be able to save others, while we get this into the right hands.' He picked up the Diadem and passed it to Zelia.

'The right hands?' she said, taking it.

'You mean... my mum?'

Amity checked the navigational cogitator. 'Why not? I need to meet this woman.'

'But we still don't know where she is.'

'Sure we do,' Talen said. 'The Emperor's Seat. Just like she told us.'

'And there is only one place we have left to search,' Mekki said. 'The planet Pastoria.'

'If it even exists,' Zelia pointed out.

Talen snorted, slipping into the co-pilot's seat. 'A minor detail. I vote we keep looking.'

'Me too,' Mekki agreed.

Zelia smiled. 'And me.'

'Then that is what we shall do,' Amity said, pulling back on a lever. 'You know, I missed having a crew...'

TO BE CONCLUDED IN
TOMB OF THE NECRON

GALACTIC COMPENDIUM

PART FIVE

THE ADEPTUS MECHANICUS

Often known as
the Adepthood of
Mars, the Adeptus
Mechanicus creates
and maintains
technology
throughout the
Imperium. Once
an empire in
its own right,
the Mechanicus
joined forces with
the Emperor of

Mankind to build a huge army that would protect the Imperium from both xenos and Chaotic threats.

The tech-adepts of the Adeptus Mechanicus augment their bodies with bionic implants and whirling mechanical arms known as mechadendrites. They follow the teachings of the Machine-Lord and believe that every cogitator contains a spirit that helps it function.

FORGE WORLDS

The Adeptus Mechanicus toil on thousands of forge worlds throughout

the Imperium. Factory planets like Aparitus are covered in vast industrial complexes that churn out weapons and vehicles for the Emperor's never-ending war against the forces of Chaos.

Their blighted landscapes are dominated by chimneys taller than the highest skyscrapers, which belch smog into the polluted air. Each manufactorum houses volcano furnaces to smelt metal while rows of servitors work day in, day out on production lines with little need for food or sleep.

THE SKITARII

The skitarii are the foot soldiers of the Adeptus Mechanicus, cybernetic warriors who have had most of their bodies replaced with

robotic parts. This doesn't mean
that they are mindless drones
like servitors, however. Capable of
independent thought, the tech-guards
are fiercely loyal and will never
give up the fight. Powered by their
cybernetic implants, skitarii can march
for months at a time without rest.

SKITARII WARGEAR

Arc Weapons – Energy weapons
powered by ancient electricity
harvested from Mars centuries ago.
Can scramble mechanical systems
or fry a xenos's brain with a single
bolt.

Cognis Flamer – A flame-thrower
governed by a machine-spirit that

can keep firing even if its user is injured or stunned.

Phosphor-Blasters – Used to mark high-priority targets on a battlefield. The knowledge of how to make these highly prized weapons has been lost over time. There is no way of knowing how many remain.

Transonic Razor – Vibrating blades that can cut through anything.

Eradication Beamer – Disintegrates its target atom by atom.

TELEPORTERS

Usually only found in voidships, teleporters require a vast amount of power to operate. They are usually used to transport troops into the midst of battle, but have special safeguards to make sure that the teleported troops don't materialise in the middle of solid rock.

There are limitations, though. Imperial teleporters can't transport anyone more than twice as tall as an average human male, and can't penetrate any wall thicker than five metres.

In the past, experiments to teleport between planets have ended in disaster, the subjects exposed to the warp. No one survived the trials, the subjects mutated beyond recognition or driven mad by the experience.

JEREMIAS

Jeremias is a high-ranking member of the Imperial Inquisition, tasked with keeping the Imperium safe against the enemies of mankind. Like all of his order, he is responsible for sniffing out corruption and dissent among citizens the galaxy over.

Immaculately furnished and clean to the point of obsession, Jeremias's ship, the *Zealot's Heart*, is as austere as its owner. Jeremias usually travels with Grimm, his faithful cyber-mastiff and Corlak, a servo-skull that acts as his personal assistant. No one but Corlak knows why Jeremias covers half his face with a metallic mask, although many believe it is to conceal a wound endured during his service to the Emperor.

CYBER-MASTIFFS

Cyber-mastiffs are robotic hounds constructed to resemble hunting dogs. Some mastiffs contain an organic component, making them cyborgs, while others – including Grimm – are completely mechanical.

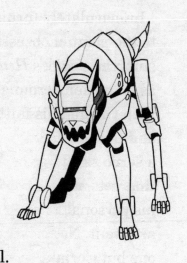

Thanks to their highly sprung legs, cyber-mastiffs can sprint at blistering speeds, and have pneumatic jaws that can bite through metal. Many are expert trackers, able to follow a scent halfway across a planet, while others work as guard dogs, protecting their owners from attack.

NURGLINGS

Little balls of snarling pus, Nurglings look like tiny bloated imps. Constantly chattering, they spread diseases wherever they scamper, causing  mischief as they chew through machinery and weaponry. They can even mash themselves together to form larger monsters.

One thing is certain: with their razor-sharp teeth, disease-ridden claws and the habit of infecting anyone they touch, Nurglings make terrible pets. Never, ever take one in!

DIFFERENT NAMES FOR NURGLINGS

The Mites of Nurgle, Tiny Plagues, Gleeful Castoffs, Little Lords, Heralds of the Unclean One.

TECHNOLOGY

While the Imperium may seem advanced, much of the machinery is a mystery to those who use or maintain it. The Adeptus Mechanicus actively punish those who deviate from the ancient blueprints that have been passed down from one generation to the next. For most humans, technology is no different to magic.

THE MACHINE-LORD

The Adeptus Mechanicus believe in an all-powerful Machine-Lord who created the technology in the universe. Officially, the adepts of Mars maintain that the Emperor is the physical embodiment of this great power, although many secretly believe that the Machine-Lord will return one day to reward his followers with fresh knowledge.

CORLAK

Jeremias's macabre drone has been by his side for as long as anyone can remember. Like all servo-skulls, Corlak is little more than a floating cogitator, but carries out the inquisitor's commands to the letter, and is even capable of piloting the *Zealot's Heart*.

No one really knows who originally owned the skull used to create Corlak. Some say it belonged to a former assistant who, on becoming seriously ill, donated his remains to the inquisitor's service. However, others have heard the rumour that the skull actually belonged to a pirate who made the mistake of attacking the inquisitor's starship while on a mission.

Only one person knows for sure – Inquisitor Jeremias himself!

ABOUT THE AUTHOR

Cavan Scott has written for such popular franchises as *Star Wars, Doctor Who, Judge Dredd, LEGO DC Super Heroes, Penguins of Madagascar, Adventure Time* and many, many more. The writer of a number of novellas and short stories set within the *Warhammer 40,000* universe, including the *Warhammer Adventures: Warped Galaxies* series, Cavan became a UK number one bestseller with his 2016 World Book Day title, *Star Wars: Adventures in Wild Space – The Escape*. Find him online at www.cavanscott.com.

ABOUT THE ARTISTS

Cole Marchetti is an illustrator and concept artist from California. When he isn't sitting in front of the computer, he enjoys hiking and plein air painting. This is his first project working with Games Workshop.

Dan Boultwood is a comic book artist and illustrator from London. When he's not drawing, he collects old shellac records and dances around badly to them in between taking forever to paint his miniatures.

STORIES FROM THE FAR FUTURE

WARPED GALAXIES

An Extract from book six
Tomb of the Necron
by Cavan Scott
(out 2021)

'What do you want?' the old woman snarled.

Zelia Lor wanted one thing and one alone – to get back to the ship. It wasn't enough that together with her friends she'd spent the last few weeks being hunted by some of the most terrifying alien races in the galaxy, now she was standing alongside Mekki and Talen in a stinking hovel, facing a wart-covered crone who wouldn't know dental hygiene if it bit her.

Grooda Vanikir was craggy-faced, snaggle-toothed and smelled worse

that a grox-paddock. Her home was a
shack, built in a waste pipe beneath
a towering hive. A waste pipe that
smelled only slightly worse than Grooda
herself.

Captain Harleen Amity stepped
forward, extending a hand in greeting,
only to retract it seconds later when
Grooda snarled like a rabid chemdog.

'I hear that you have certain...
abilities,' the rogue trader said.

Grooda's bloodshot eyes narrowed.
'What if I do?'

Amity produced a bulging purse that
jangled as she waved it in front of
the woman. 'Then you'll end the day
considerably richer than you started it.'

Grooda shot out a bony hand to grab
the proffered bounty, only for the rogue
trader to snatch the purse away.

'You'll be paid after you've told us
what we want to know.'